EMOTIONALLY UNSTABLE

First Edition

Published by Fairies and Fantasy Pty Ltd 2019

Paperback ISBN: 978-0-6485427-7-3

Hardcover ISBN: 978-1-922390-13-4

www.selinafenech.com

EMOTIONALLY UNSTABLE

THE EMPATH 2 CHRONICLES

SELINA A. FENECH

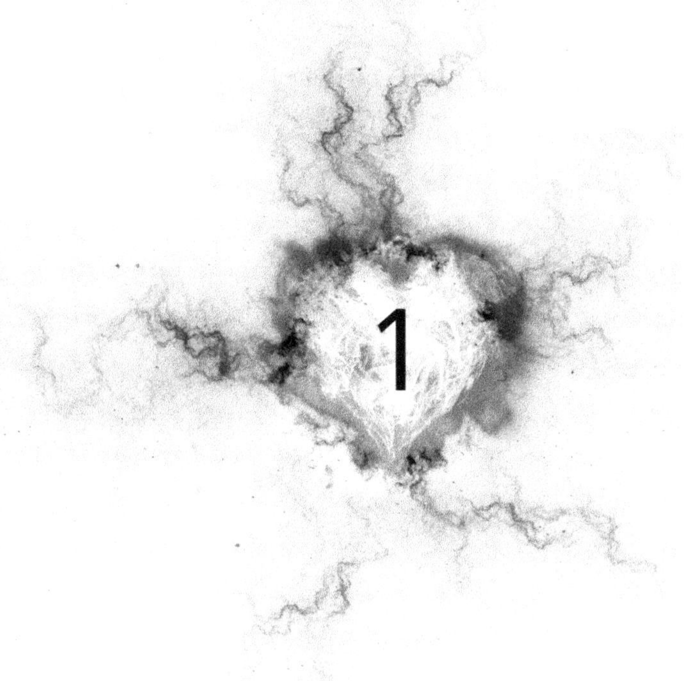

I t was funny how little I knew about Dean.

In the chaos of what had happened to us—discovering empaths and our powers and almost getting killed—I had grown to feel so much for him, but I didn't even know his last name until I saw it on his hospital chart. Dean Lasslow. And he was apparently eighteen, a year older than me. When Mom and Dad agreed to let him stay out our place for a while, they started making arrangements and it turned out he'd dropped out of school halfway through his final year to work. As soon as Mom learned that, she got straight to action and enrolled Dean at my school so he could graduate with me. Apparently, there was no way I was using any of the recent events as an excuse to skip my normal education.

Dean left hospital with strict orders not to lift anything heavy or perform strenuous exercise. He was given a huge list of post-hospital-care instructions about how to change the dressings on his wounds, plus a large paper bag full of medication, and that was pretty much it. He had almost none of his own belongings with him.

Mom and Dad had offered to pick up some of Dean's things for him, but he didn't want them having to deal with his dad on their own, so it was agreed we would all go by his place together to pack before heading back to my home.

Mom pulled up the hire car in front of Dean's trailer. Down the laneway, surrounded by trash and weeds, some unsupervised kids were smashing bottles for fun, and a cloud of anger and depression drifted to me from the untended homes around us. Dad reached over and held Mom's hand. I knew her childhood hadn't been great, but she kept most of the details from me. She always preferred to focus on the positive. But from the way Dad moved so quickly to reassure her now, and the dark blue chill of sadness that surrounded her, I wondered how many of her childhood memories were being relived. I wanted to hug her for any pain she was feeling, and for who she turned out to be despite it all.

"Wait here. I'll be right back," Dean said. He stepped gingerly out of the car, the still-healing bullet wound making such movement difficult. I wanted to hug him too.

Dean didn't even make it to the front door before it flew open, metal screen clattering against the side of the trailer home. His dad burst out, like he'd been standing there waiting the entire time Dean had been in hospital. Standing there waiting, and drinking.

Dean had left his car door open, and we could hear every slurry word.

"Gone f'weeks, and look at you—nothing wrong with you. Think you're just waltzing back in after the trouble you caused? Sending cops banging down my door?" His shirt was stained, and he had an almost empty bottle of bourbon in one hand.

"I'm just here to collect my things," Dean said coolly. He took another step and his dad blocked his path, thrusting out a palm against Dean's shoulder.

I was out of my seat so fast the car was left rocking in my wake. My parents were right behind me. After they got over the impact of the shuddering car.

"Leaving me again? Good. Sick of you stealing my paycheck."

"Mr. Lasslow!" Mom yelled.

"He's not stealing anything; he's just picking up some clothes," Dad said in the calm voice of someone trying to defuse a situation. Then he seemed to rethink the whole plan and addressed Dean. "Maybe we can pick you up some basics at a store for now, come back another time for the rest."

Dean's dad stepped right up in front of Dean. Dean flinched away from his breath. "Weaseled yourself a real sugar-mama family to look after you, huh? Too good for this place now?"

Dean breathed out slowly, and in the calmest voice, said, "I'll just get some things and be right back."

He tried to sidestep into the trailer, but his dad grabbed the shoulder of his too-large charity T-shirt and wrenched him backwards.

I was there in a flash. I rebalanced Dean as gently as I could to stop him from stumbling over. I didn't want to know what a rough fall would do to his healing internal organs. I stood between him and his Dad, ready for anything.

Or I thought I was, until Dean's dad spat in my face.

My jaw dropped and I wanted to vomit. I wiped frantically at the slippery ooze on my chin.

"Little whore, stealing my only family from me," he growled.

Anger fired through me. Mom and Dad rushed to my side, and it took their strength combined to drag me back to the car, even with Dean blocking my full powers.

"We're leaving. Now," Mom said, and Dean followed us.

I was shaking with fury, and heartbroken for Dean, that all the family he had left in the world was that disaster of a parent. Dean deserved so much more. "We can't just go. What about your stuff?" I said to him.

Dean looked back at the rusty, gray trailer surrounded by monstrous weeds, and his drunk dad, waving his arms and yelling obscenities at us. "There's nothing there I need."

We all took our seats again and Mom started the engine. The gravel road crunched as the car started rolling away.

"Well," he added, "except my motorbike."

"Your *what?*" I turned back, surprised, and caught the glimpse of a wheel of what could have been a motorbike around one corner of the trailer.

"It's just an old dirt bike. My mate was borrowing it when you visited before. But if I leave it there any longer, Dad will probably sell it."

My mom turned halfway around from watching the road. "Would your friend be willing to bring it to Bellscroft to our place for you?"

Dean watched out the window quietly as we drove away from the trailer park. "Yeah, yeah he might."

Dean called his friend and made arrangements in a series of short monosyllable sounds. His phone and wallet, all he'd had in his pockets when we ended up in hospital, were all he had of his own now.

The drive was silent for a long time after that. The emotions flowing off my parents ranged from angry to sad to worried then back to angry. Dean remained his unreadable, cold self.

The trip took an uncomfortable two hours. On the way, we stopped at a strip mall that had a budget department store draped in 'clearance sale' signs. My mom mumbled about the ridiculously cheap clothing prices and unfair work conditions in Bangladesh, but begrudgingly agreed it would do for now. Dean picked out some basics, plain T-shirts and jeans, a hoodie and underwear, deodorant and a toothbrush, socks and a pair of sneakers. He checked every price tag and mouthed a running total to keep track. He picked the cheapest every time and didn't seem fussy about what he bought, unlike the kind of dramas I'd pulled in the past about what my wardrobe should include.

At the checkout, Dean pulled out some of the cash remaining from the sale of my necklace, my 'wages' to him when he couldn't work because of me. He checked and counted out how much he had left before he tried to pay.

But my parents weren't having it and Dean wouldn't accept them paying, and it quickly turned into a scene. I couldn't call it an argument, Dean was being too polite for that, but a large queue of impatient customers was building up behind us.

Mom took Dean by the wrist and led him away from the checkout. From the look on her face and the fountain of red and orange emotional energy flowing from her, I wasn't going with them, and neither did Dad. We just helped push our purchases to the side so other customers could move through around our drama.

Over beside a rack of magazines and gum, Mom had crouched down in front of Dean, looking up at him as she talked with the most intense expression on her face. There was some conversation back and forth. I tried to imagine what she was saying to break through his pride and let them help him. Had she ever been in a similar situation?

Dean seemed to be standing firm on something, and soon, I saw Mom yield to him. But he must have also yielded to her, because when they came back, Mom paid for his clothes and other items.

On the way out Mom pulled through a drive-through liquor store and picked up a six-pack of beer, which Dean paid for.

"What ... what?" I stuttered.

"*These,*" Mom said, emphasizing the word, "will be staying in our possession until the necessary time."

I looked across at Dean for an explanation, but he was staring the other way, out the window.

When we finally pulled up out the front of our house, I couldn't believe how happy I was to see it. I was almost ready to jump out of the car and start kissing the garden path.

Home. It felt like so long since I'd been there. All my stuff. My room. My parents. All where we were meant to be.

Inside, everything had been cleaned up after the quake, and the section of living room which had the crack running down it had been repaired but not yet repainted, the white plaster stark against the smoky lavender walls.

My parents showed Dean to his room, which was really Dad's office with a sofa bed in it.

"Showers are three minutes or less, and hang your towel in your room to re-use a couple of times before washing it." Dad was rattling off his list of green-living house rules. Water conservation, recycling, low power habits. I was used to it all, but Dean listened carefully like it was life or death. If I didn't know better, I'd say he looked nervous.

"Yes, Mr. Mirawi," he said for about the fifth time in a row.

"Once the hire car is returned, there's no car, so Livvy can help you get used to the bus-and-train routine around here. Curfew for getting home is ten p.m. unless otherwise discussed."

"Yes, Mr. Mirawi."

"And we also have one new rule," he said, looking at me now. "A new curfew. Neither of you are to be in the other's room after dinnertime, and no closed doors at any time you're alone together in a room."

Dean didn't reply. He shot me a look.

"Daaad." I blushed. "We're not …"

Mom gave me a no-nonsense look and I knew her no-nonsense attitude was about to embarrass me. "We've talked about relationships and sex before love, and we do trust you to look after your own body. But you've both just been through a very traumatic time, and brains don't always work their best after trauma. The new curfew is temporary, but it will be strictly enforced until our lives start coming back into the realm of reality."

"Okay, Mom, okay." My blush grew hotter all the way to my ears.

We gave Dean some time to settle in on his own and unpack the couple of shopping bags worth of new belongings into the side cupboard Dad had cleared out for him. I went and lay down on my own bed and cuddled my own pillow and cried in relief.

It wasn't long before the doorbell rang. I answered, and a guy was standing there with two helmets, rechecking his phone and our house number. Behind him on the street was a banged up dirt bike.

Dean stepped up behind me, and introduced his friend Mako. I stood back and let them have a chat. Mako seemed highly amused by the whole situation, and especially pleased with getting to 'heist' the bike out from under Dean's dad's nose. Mom and Dad appeared with the six-pack and it all made sense. It was payment for bike delivery. Payment Dean wanted to make himself. On top of that, Dean used what I figured was the last of his cash to pay for his mate's public transport home.

Dad wheeled the bike into the garage which was otherwise used as a second storeroom for Duck Egg Blue stock. Then we all stood at the door and waved goodbye to Mako, something he found very funny.

Once he'd walked off to the bus stop, I exhaled a few weeks' worth of stress. That was it. All sorted. Time to just settle back into my life and get back to normal, if that were even remotely possible.

"It's nice to be home," I said softly.

Mom made a sucking noise through her teeth. "Just one

more new house rule, though."

I sighed, knowing I was in no position to debate parental authority right now. "Sure, what is it?"

"You're not to go on that bike."

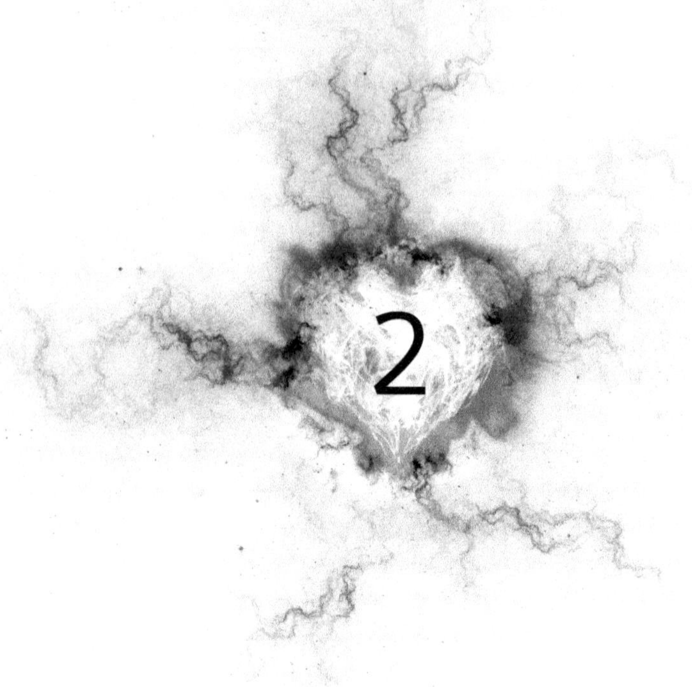

2

D ean put his hand on my shoulder to steady me.
We edged closer.

"I was wrong. I'm not ready," I mumbled. Energy flooded me, like overactive bees humming through my veins. It already felt like it could drive me crazy.

"You can do it. You're strong."

We took another step closer to the school gates.

"Oof. Do you think you can ramp up your blocking amount at all?"

Dean shook his head. "Not really. I think if I try and do much more it will be getting into the territory of shutting down your powers for good."

I looked at the crowd of teenagers moving around the school yard. Their emotions felt like a thick cloud, surrounding me. I couldn't even clearly define them, just this rainbow-swirl mass of intense *feeling*. I felt like I could either punch a hole through a brick wall or suddenly take off flying—*if* my brain didn't spontaneously combust first.

"Okay." I took a deep breath. "Here we go."

We made it in through the gates and were heading up the gum-spotted concrete path to the main building to take Dean to the office when I heard a long, high-pitched sound.

"Liiiivyyyy!"

Even the pressure in my head couldn't stop me from being excited.

"Natiiiiiiiiiii!" I squealed back.

She appeared like magic from behind a group of kids exchanging class notes, and ran towards me in pretend slow motion. A huge toothy smile shone on her dark skin and her ringlets bounced in perfect rhythm along with her.

I opened my arms for a hug, laughing at her dramatics, but she stopped short a couple of steps from me and changed to a pouting, hands-on-hips stance.

"Where *were* you?" she accused. "You disappear for weeks

and not a single call or message or So-Snap?"

We had a plan for this situation. Me and my parents had decided that if I shared anything about what had happened, it would be exactly the same story I'd told the police. Consistency was everything, since we figured some news might have spread already. Nati seemed completely clueless though, and I wondered, maybe vainly, whether anything about what had happened to Dean and I had made the news at all. It didn't seem that way, which was odd.

I was only just opening my mouth when Nati started up again.

"You've been sick, haven't you? Wow, look at you—you look like the walking dead, babe. It's not contagious, right?"

I half smiled. I did feel pretty awful. Dealing with the relentless level of heightened emotions was taking a lot out of me. I felt clammy and jittery, and hoped Nati didn't jump from sickness to just-out-of-rehab with her assumptions. "It's not catching; don't worry. I'll give you the whole story soon."

"Oh. My. Smosh." Nati's eyes widened as she *noticed* Dean. "And who are you?"

"D-"

"You little con-artist!" Nati interrupted, turning back to me with the slyest expression. Man, I didn't realize how much I'd missed her, and this display of pure Nati was making me giggle. "Pretending like you've been off sick and coming back to school with a honey at your side? You've got some insane-level spillage to do!"

"I know. I'll catch you all up soon. Cross my heart. Last period, chemistry?"

"It's a date." She grinned. "Are you around for good, new guy?"

Nati, you've no idea how complicated that question is. "Dean's enrolled. He'll probably be here for a bit."

"That's bonkers!" she shouted. Dean and I looked at each other, confused. "Two new guys in one week! The other guy, Ash? I have to say, he's easy on the libido as well. Oh, oh!"

She ducked in close to me and lifted her chin like a pointer to the corner of the red-brick building. "There he is, and he's totally looking at you!"

I peeked over my shoulder, and saw him. An Asian boy with bleached white hair really was looking straight at me. He caught me looking and I averted my eyes, then looked at Dean, who had his eyebrows very slightly raised. I shrugged. Not like I had control over who was looking at me.

"What is this? Livvy love week? Is it this new waif look you're rocking that's got the boys flocking?" Nati said with a little shimmy of her hips.

I was saved from any further embarrassment by the bell.

I hugged Nati quickly and promised again to chat in chemistry.

"Your face is chemistry!" she yelled gleefully as we headed off in different directions.

Dean and I made our way to the office and dealt with both his introduction to the school and my recent absence from it. My parents had sorted most of it out; there were just forms and timetables, homework and textbooks to pick up before getting to our classes, all of which had been arranged for Dean and I to be together, which couldn't have been easy. But Dad did a large share of volunteering for the school so he had favors he could call on. Dean got a photo taken for his student card and would have to pick it up in the afternoon.

He was looking unsure about the whole being-back-at-school thing. And I knew he was here mostly for my benefit, but I hoped he would get something out of it too. I mean, it was high school, but it was a good high school with some good kids and teachers I even liked, like Mr. Jones, who we had first up that morning for history.

As we walked into the class, Mr. Jones tapped me on the shoulder and said, "Glad you're back. Was worried when you disappeared on us that night."

"Sorry about that. I hope my parents explained everything." I ducked past before he could reply, and took a seat near the middle of the room next to an empty desk for Dean. He paused to introduce himself to the teacher and hand over some paperwork.

Ash slipped right into what should have been Dean's chair. *Ugh. I should have put something on it to claim it.* I wasn't thinking straight with the rainbow of emotional auras creating a haze in the room, including the bright sunshine yellow beaming from Ash as he grinned at me.

I shot Dean a look of apology as he moved to another available desk behind me.

It was still close enough to get a decent blocking effect, but I silently cursed Ash for meaning I couldn't have Dean at my side.

He didn't seem to notice and, still smiling, started talking in a strong Australian accent. "Hey, you new to this place too? I'm Ash."

"Livvy," I said, busy getting my textbooks in order. "And I'm not new. Just been away for a while."

"Yeah? Where to? On holiday?" His grin stayed large. He was as cheery as a kid's TV host. He glowed almost too bright to look at.

I rubbed my forehead and turned to the front of the classroom, trying to make a point of paying attention to Mr. Jones who had begun the lesson on the smart board. Something about an assassination causing World War I. I was behind on the details there. I glanced to the side and Ash was still staring at me, waiting for an answer.

"In hospital," I hissed.

"Whoa. What happened?" He sat sideways on his chair to face me better and looked me up and down, as if seeking clues as to my illness or injury. "Was it serious?"

I shot him a glare. Was he trying to get us both in trouble? Why so many questions? Maybe I could have avoided an interrogation if I'd lied and said I had been on vacation, but that wasn't the plan. Stick to the script. Stay consistent. Or just avoid giving busy-bodies any unnecessary information entirely.

"I'm fine now. Shh." I tilted my head to Mr. Jones who seemed to have noticed our conversation. I had my pen in hand, trying to take notes, but between Ash's prying and the distracting buzz of emotions swarming through my body like angry ants, I was having trouble concentrating.

"You look knackered. Sure you're not still feeling a bit off? Or is it because it's so cold in here?" Ash continued looking straight at me. Like he was oblivious to the rest of the room. Or to me being annoyed. Or the increasingly bewildered teacher who stared right at him, tapping his foot.

"Ash Len," Mr. Jones snapped. "Private conversations are for outside the classroom. If you feel the need to talk so much, maybe you can go have a chat to the principal.”

“Sorry, Mr. Jones,” he said, his cheery grin still in place. “I’m just so excited to be in this new school, with so many interesting new people to meet.”

Confused laughter swept across the room, as though the class was unsure if this guy was trying to be a clown or not.

Mr. Jones also looked bewildered at Ash’s behavior. It seemed almost arrogant or cheeky, like he was the kind of person used to getting away with anything. His comment about it being cold popped back up in my memory’s ear. *Huh.* I narrowed my eyes, my suspicions twitching.

Mr. Jones cleared his throat. “Well, some more interest in the lesson would be appreciated.”

“Sure thing, mate,” Ash said, turning himself to the front of the room again, pen in hand, head down.

He didn’t talk to me again for the rest of the lesson, but every time I glanced across at him, he was also glancing right back at me from under his straight white hair. Grinning. Not taking any notes.

The school bus stop was a swell of jostling teenage bodies, wired from a day in school and ready to be free. A couple of supervising teachers near the gates kept trying to remind us to stay calmly in our bus lines but it was futile. Between the hot tin roof and the concrete floor, students dueled in games of handball or huddled together, streaming funny videos on their phones or taking selfies. In the corners farthest from the teachers, couples pressed their bodies together, making out or just staring dreamily into each other's eyes.

My gaze drifted up to Dean beside me. He stood close, with his shoulder pressed against mine, but there wasn't that intimacy or rush of lust between us that the other teenage couples seemed to have. At least not in the Dean-to-Livvy direction. In the Livvy-to-Dean direction, just a glimpse of those intense gray eyes made my whole body whimper. But I held back, uncertainty a wall of ice between us. Were we even a couple? Was it always going to be this hard to know how Dean was feeling? Would I always doubt us?

Dean caught me staring, and without saying a word, he wrapped his hand around mine. *There he goes being a mind reader again.* But Mom always did say I had a face like an open book.

His hand felt good in mine, and the flutters in my heart grew fierce as a tornado.

"You two are so cute together. Like Romeo and Juliet, except ones who kicked death in the ass!" Nati had proclaimed during chemistry class. She had gasped all the way through my explanation of my absence, how I'd gotten caught up with a gang, the bank robbery, and the fact Dean had been shot. Gasps were punctuated with a lot of 'No way!' and 'Shut up!' She ate up every detail, her eyes sparkling with a fierce, protective awe.

After class, it was like she didn't want to let me out of her sight, offering to drive us both home even though it was out of her way. I declined, happy to catch the bus and return to normal routines.

Our bus pulled up out the front of the gates, and kids started filing into line, pushing through the rest of the swirling crowd of students to get on. Just before reaching the gate, Dean's hand slipped out of mine and another student pushed in between us. Then my wrist was grabbed again from behind. A sharp tug pulled me out of line.

"Hey, Livvy! It's Livvy, isn't it? I've met so many people today, it's a bit of a blur." Ash grinned at me. He let go of my wrist and I just nodded to him, trying to head back to the bus as the last student in line got on.

He grabbed my shoulder and stopped me from walking away. I knew I was stronger than him, but didn't want him to also know that, so I let him get away with it. "Ash, I have to go."

"I wanted to ask you something," he persisted.

"Dude, that's my bus," I snapped at him.

I heard the *whoosh* of the bus doors closing. I turned to find Dean, and spotted him on the bus as it pulled away. Without me.

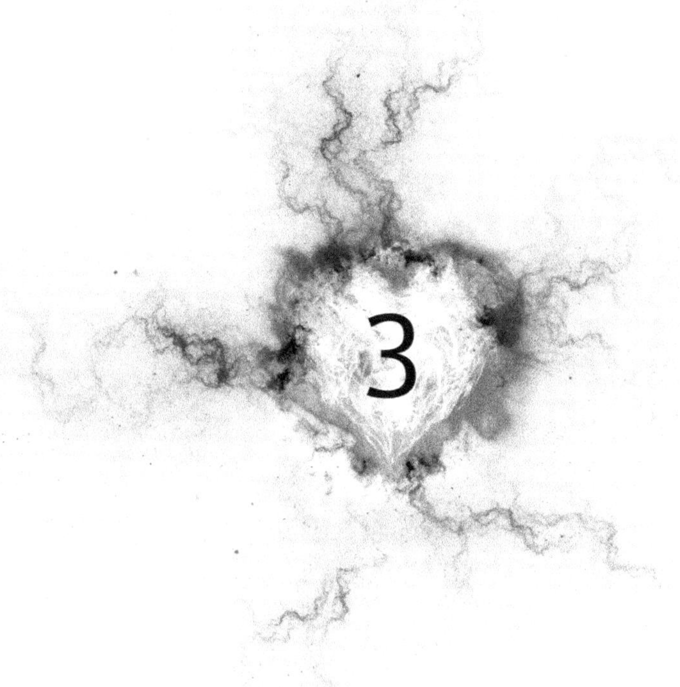

3

Dean stood in the aisle of the bus. He'd noticed I wasn't behind him anymore, and looked out the window. Our eyes met, both wide with fear.

Down around the back of the covered bus shelter, I heard raised voices, as a couple of girls started pushing each other around. The buzz of emotions from my fellow classmates was building up in me. *Fast.* I had to get to Dean. I really didn't want to be seizuring out in front of everyone on my first day back at school. Or at all.

Ash still held my shoulder, saying something I wasn't paying any attention to.

I stepped out of Ash's grip, pushing him back at the same time, and left him stumbling with a look of sheer astonishment on his face.

I ducked quickly between the other students, sidestepping behind some larger bodies until I was out of sight of Ash and any watching teachers, then slipped away behind the covered shelter walls.

The street was visible through the thick bars of the school fence, and a row of busses had stopped just outside, waiting for the green light. My bus was one of them.

I had to get to it. And I had to do it without totally revealing my powers.

I dashed to a section of fence where bushes grew on either side, hoping they'd be enough to obscure the view if anyone was watching me run around the schoolyard like a weirdo.

Giving the fence a calculating glare, I ran straight at it. I moved fast—there was obviously enough fear around for me to use. I hoped there was also enough anger, so I'd have the strength to make the jump. I judged my moment and leaped. The tops of the metal bars skimmed the soles of my shoes. Dirt swirled as I landed behind the leafy bush, feet firm and heart pounding.

But the bus was already pulling away again, down the street.

I ran along not far behind, trying to keep out of direct view of people on the street and the vehicle's windows. Thank goodness school was in a quiet part of town. I ducked behind parked cars then sprinted ahead in a blur of speed when the coast was clear. It wasn't hard keeping up with the bus at first, but I knew just around the corner they'd be moving into a faster speed zone and I wasn't sure if I'd make that pace while staying covert. I needed to get in the bus.

Or maybe *on* the bus …

Just around the corner was a billboard truck that had been there for months, advertising a new dental surgery. I just hoped they hadn't moved it.

I rounded the corner, anxiously scanning for it and—*there.* Yes! It was still there. The slope of the double-sided A-frame billboard was steeper than I'd remembered, almost straight up and down. My shoes had basic rubber soles that I hoped would give me enough traction, because this was my last chance to get on the bus, and not get a seizure in the gutter.

I gunned it, using every bit of speed and strength I could muster. It felt like I was running at a wall, but when I reached it, I scrambled up the face of the white-toothed grinning woman on the ad, toes and hands moving together to pull me up to the top. And there was the bus in front of me, just in front of me and starting to accelerate.

I didn't slow down. I pushed off with both feet and sprang from the top of the billboard, my hair flying about as the world disappeared from under me. My chest tightened. *I'm up in the air.* It was amazing. And terrifying. *Please let me come down in the right place.*

I landed neatly on top of the bus in a crouched action pose, and couldn't help but smile.

I did it. Now *that* was superhero stuff. I felt like I had flown through the sky, and my heart raced faster than I had.

I dropped down onto my stomach. It wouldn't pay to have anyone see a teenage girl riding a bus around like a skateboard. After catching my breath, I slid over to the edge, ducking down to look through a window. Dean stood up the front. He seemed to be arguing with the bus driver who waved him back, probably telling him to take a seat. With the bus on its way, it wouldn't come back for students who'd missed it, or let anyone off outside of a designated stop.

The other students seemed too involved in their own conversations or phones to be looking my way, so I took a chance and waved to get Dean's attention.

Halfway through a sentence, his eyes turned my way and he stopped, mouth open. I grinned, giving him a thumbs up.

He said something else to the driver then took a seat, eyebrows raised at my upside-down face.

Another kid turned my way, and I moved out of sight. I took off my backpack and flipped over onto my back to watch the blue sky for the rest of the ride home, pretending I was still flying.

When the bus pulled up on our street, I waited for Dean to get off, and then jumped down off the back of the bus as it left, landing out of sight behind a gray van.

"What happened?" Dean came over to me. "I thought you were right behind me, getting on the bus. Then you weren't. I tried to get them to stop but the driver wouldn't listen."

"I know. It's okay, I was held up by someone, but did you see me? I was so fast, like *so* fast, and I jumped onto a fleeping bus. Right onto it!" My empath powers had calmed again now I was beside Dean, but my heart and mind were still in crazy-excited mode. "I went full superhero."

We started the walk up the street to my house, and I skipped around Dean as he half-smiled at my enthusiasm.

"I don't know if I've ever run like that before. Or jumped! Or landed! Do you know how I landed? Not on my face! It was like POW." I demonstrated by jumping a little on the spot and landing in an action pose.

"You are such a huge dork." But Dean smiled, as though he really liked it.

Mom met us at the front door. I bet she'd been hovering. She knew I'd been worried about my first day back at school. "How was it?" she asked.

I tried to contain my grin. Pure nonchalance. "It was fine. No dramas at all."

I rapped my knuckles lightly against Dean's door. Mom and Dad were watching a movie in the living room downstairs. Dean and I were meant to be catching up on homework before bed. Separately, in our own rooms, because it was after dinner.

I'd had a soothing bath and changed into pajamas and tried to relax and just focus on studying.

But the excitement of today still zipped through my veins. I couldn't stop thinking about the race I'd run, the sensation of flying, and the way Dean had held my hand in the bus shelter. So I had fearlessly snuck down the hallway, desperate to see Dean to have someone to share those feelings with.

I heard some shuffling but the door didn't open. I didn't dare knock louder, so I pushed the sliding door open a crack and peeked in. Dean was sitting cross-legged on the sofa bed, wearing only gray sweat-pants, reading a paperback.

My breath caught and my cheeks heated. I almost backed away, but Dean looked up and rested the book on the bed, like a sign it was okay for me to interrupt. I stepped in and closed the door behind me, careful not to make a sound.

"Isn't this against the rules?" he whispered.

I answered by grinning mischievously and wriggling my eyebrows.

Dean didn't share my delinquent delight. He reached across and grabbed a shirt, pulling it on quickly. "I don't want to get in trouble off your parents."

"I just wanted to chat." My enthusiasm dropped quickly. For all I could tell, Dean didn't want me there. But I could never really tell what he wanted, or if he wanted. *What would this situation be like with a normal boy?*

I almost bit my tongue. *Normal?* I'd never been the type to want normal.

I sat next to Dean and studied his face, his skin smooth and pale like no laugh lines had ever marred it. Those gray eyes looked like they could be thunderstorms but held none of that wild energy.

I could never sense his emotions. What he was feeling. If he felt at all. But I knew his heart. I'd once felt the pain he held so deep in there. I knew his kindness. I knew he felt *something* for me. It was just hard to tell exactly what and how much when he didn't show it.

I found myself lost for words after having just said I wanted to chat. *Ugh, so awkward.* I picked up the book he was reading. It was a space opera classic, probably off one of the shelves in the room. One of Dad's favorites. "You like reading?"

"Yeah. It helps me shut out the things around me, to escape." He coughed softly. "And it was easy to find cheap second-hand paperbacks back at home."

"Paperbacks? Haven't you discovered e-books yet? You can borrow my e-reader if you want since I mostly read on my phone. I have so many books in my collection," I said as my mind served up the image of Dean's tiny trailer room. Even his phone looked pre-smart-phone era. He had been working to support himself and his alcoholic dad, and there I was, boasting about my e-book collection and how many devices I had. Including the brand-new phone my parents had given me while I was in hospital since my own phone had been left behind and the one Jake got me had become evidence. Me, who had been so excited by the idea of affluence and opulence that I got involved with criminals.

Thankfully, Dean didn't seem as mortified by me at that

moment as I was. He just said, "Sure, sounds good," as I tried to get my brain functioning in an acceptable way.

My life had changed so much. My eyes had been opened so wide, I felt like I didn't know how to exist anymore. Like I couldn't be the person I used to be. But my identity hadn't quite caught up with that memo yet, hadn't grown into it. I was a toddler wearing her dad's Superman costume.

And then there was Dean, who made me want to be worthy of a love he might never be able to express. How was I supposed to act around him?

My mind was muddled. What had originally been planned as a fun secret meet-up was turning into a confusing mess. What had I wanted, really, when I snuck down here?

"Are you," I started, hesitantly, "having trouble feeling normal again?"

Dean's eyes were on mine, and I wondered if he'd been studying my face the way I had his. "Yeah. I'm not sure how normal I ever felt, but yeah, I know I've changed, from who I was before all this. You?"

I bit my lip and nodded. "And it's not just the powers. I mean, it's hard to feel normal when you have super strength and speed, and who knows what else. But other things too. I feel … different. In a good way, but also a way I just don't know how to make work yet."

Dean nodded.

We sat in silence and I considered reaching out and taking his hand, or leaning my head on his shoulder. Instead, I reached over and placed my palm on his shirt, so gently it was barely a touch at all. Through the thin material, I felt the plasticky square of post-op dressing covering his bullet wound. The action moved us closer. Dean's breath ghosted over my cheek.

I whispered, "Are you feeling a bit better?"

"Yeah." Dean looked down at my hand. "I was worried about you on the bus today. When you didn't get on, I just kept imagining you on the ground, hurting."

The pain I'd felt when I saw Dean on the ground, shot and bleeding, was far greater than a seizure had ever caused me. But maybe that was how he felt now, knowing what happened to me when he wasn't close by my side. "I'm sorry that you have to be here for me all the time now."

"I really don't mind. Honestly, I'm not sure my life was really going anywhere before. Or, I mean, I don't think I had it in me to want my life to go anywhere." He turned back to look at me and the edges of his eyes were just slightly red, the only hint of emotion on his face. "I think all I was doing was ... existing. You, and being here for you, has given me something to care about again."

I exhaled softly as though trying to release the butterflies from my stomach. "And is that okay? Caring about something again?"

Dean shook his head just the smallest bit. "It hurts. But in a good way. It means I'm feeling *something* again, when I haven't felt anything in so long."

A single small tear spilled over my eyelid, surprising me, then I surprised myself again when my lips met Dean's. The kiss was soft at first, until I pushed harder, seeking, and his mouth opened under mine. He wrapped his arms around me, pulling me up into his lap, holding me tight, and pressing my chest against his.

The *flutter-flutter* in my heart was no longer gentle. It raged with a burning intensity and all I could sense was Dean and the kiss and his hands and his tongue, and that was all I wanted.

But the intensity kept growing. Too fast. Too strong. A pounding in my head and electricity in my veins. Fire in my muscles. The world grew blurry and dark. I clung to Dean's T-shirt and heard it rip as he backed away from me, pushing me off him onto the bed where I fell, close to convulsing.

"Livvy? Liv? Are you okay?" He was leaning over me, a hand on my forehead. I blinked my vision clear to see his expression blank and calm again, and my body started coming back under control.

"How did that go so wrong?" I grunted.

"I'm sorry." Dean helped me sit up on the edge of the bed, and crouched in front of me. He held my hands and looked at them instead of my face. His words were measured and his voice monotone, as though he were doing everything he could to remain emotionless. "I couldn't keep my blocking power going. When I was kissing you. The way I feel about you … I couldn't control it. And I hurt you."

"You didn't hurt me. It isn't your fault I'm like this." I could have cried. I'd wanted proof that Dean felt something for me, and I got it, right along with a clear message of *no, you can't eat the cake too*. The rollercoaster of the last five minutes had left me teary and frustrated. "What does this mean? Can we never kiss or …?"

"I don't know."

"But do you want to? Kiss me, I mean?" It seemed like the wrong question to be asking. But I wanted to. Despite what had happened, I still wanted to be kissing Dean right then, to have my arms around him and be with him, in a way that felt like I was *with* him. I wanted to know what our relationship was and have all the good things that came with connection. Like kissing.

"I don't think we can. Not until we find a way to fix your powers. I don't want to hurt you again," he said eventually, perhaps reluctantly.

I just nodded. He was right. I had to do something to fix myself. I couldn't live like this forever. Even with him right there, I could still sense emotions around me so clearly, like I could almost tell how everyone on the street was feeling. Including two angry bodies just outside the door.

Oh, butts. We were busted.

4

I slipped back out of Dean's room and closed the door behind me so that whatever happened next didn't have to involve him.

"Olivia Poppy Mirawi," Dad said, sternly.

Ouch. I knew it was serious when my parents full-named me.

They both stood there, arms crossed. Mom glanced at Dean's closed door, and beckoned me to follow her with a flick of her chin.

I obediently shuffled along behind them, glad they didn't give me an earful right there where Dean could hear everything through his door. In horror, I wondered how much my parents had heard through that same door.

On the way down the stairs, I looked out the window onto the dark street below, and noticed an unmarked gray van out the front. It looked like the same one I had landed behind when getting off the bus. *A surveillance van?* In the past, I'd write that off as my imagination being its wild self, but these days, I wasn't so sure. I thought about mentioning it to my parents, but they'd think I was just trying to deflect. I filed it away with my suspicions about Ash to review at a later time, under the heading 'When did I become so paranoid?' My imagination used to feed me budding romance plots at every turn, and now I was seeing enemies in every corner.

Once in the kitchen, Dad pulled out a stool at the counter for me and Mom started making herself a cup of tea. I could sense the anger in both of them, but they were clearly restraining it.

"I'm sorry. I know it was past bedroom curfew. It was entirely my fault; I went to him. I just wanted to talk to him." At first, at least, until the kissing started.

"You're only sorry because you got caught," Mom pointed out. She slowly dunked her teabag as she placed her cup on the counter, then sat down across from me. "And I understand. You wanted to spend some time with him and didn't think that our rules were important to follow. But you know we put rules in place for a reason."

Dad stayed standing up, behind Mom. "Look, we remember what it's like to be a teenager, and the feelings that come with it. We also remember that teenagers don't always think straight, and make mistakes like sneaking into a boy's room when they've been told not to. So you're getting a free pass on this one. This. One. Time."

Phew?

Dad opened his mouth as if to speak again. No, they weren't finished yet. Not phew.

"It's not that we don't want you following your heart or having sex," Mom said in a matter-of-fact way that left my jaw on the counter. "We'd prefer you to be having sex under our roof where we know you're safe and making the right choices, rather than sneaking off somewhere less safe."

"Mooom," I gasped.

"Normally," Dad added. "But these aren't normal times. You know that, right?"

I nodded. I really, really knew that. But now wasn't the time to let them know I wouldn't be kissing Dean again anytime soon because of what it did to me.

Dad tilted his head, his anger shifting to sympathy. "Lollipop, you kids have been through some serious trauma. You can't trust what your bodies or minds are telling you right now.

That's why we have to set these boundaries. And stick to them."

"That's also why," Mom said, looking down at her darkening tea, but still not drinking it, "we've made an appointment for you and Dean to go and see a therapist."

"You think we're crazy?" I squeaked.

"No, of course not," Dad said. He came over to stand beside me, and put his arm around my shoulders. "We believe you. We know what you've experienced is real. That's the whole point. You need help dealing with what has happened. Gaining superpowers, challenging your entire view of reality—it's kind of a big deal, dear."

"Having someone professional to talk to about things can be really helpful for anyone. Counselling will help you understand how you're really feeling when all your feelings seem to blend into a confusing mess."

I didn't like the idea. It felt like a betrayal, despite them saying they believed me. It felt like they were saying I was broken, or wrong, and that I needed fixing. Defensively, I muttered, "What I need is to find a way to control my powers. Will they be able to help with that? Can I even tell them about my powers or will they lock me up?"

Mom and Dad looked at each other. "You'll have to skirt around the superpowers detail. We still think it's best that stays between us, professional confidentiality or otherwise. But they still might be able to help you. You said your powers are based on emotions, and who better to help you understand emotions than a therapist?"

I nodded begrudgingly. Maybe there was something to it. I had no other plans yet on how to even start getting my powers under control. It wasn't like my parents could find an empath specialist to send me to. They had to find the next best thing. They were trying their hardest. I was just too riled up to appreciate it.

"Okay. Fine. I'll go. I guess it might be good for Dean, too. In other ways."

I wondered if he'd ever had counseling when his mother got sick and died. I doubted it. All their family's money had gone to her medical care; there probably wasn't anything left for Dean.

And maybe a counselor could help me get my powers under control. Maybe there was a cure there. Was that what my parents wanted after all? Maybe they thought I could be cured entirely, and go back to being their normal girl again.

But there was no going back for me. I had changed.

Forever.

5

The next day at school brought with it another history class, and another lesson with Ash. He was hovering near the door when Dean and I arrived, and I made sure Dean got a seat right beside me this time. I was still sour at Ash for making me miss the bus. Whether he'd meant it or not, he'd caused a risky situation. So far, no one had come up to me at school to ask why I could run at super-speed though, so fingers crossed on that front.

Ash followed us over, and I smiled when another girl, Roxy, took the remaining seat on my other side. But then Ash outright asked if he could swap with her.

I tried to signal her with a shake of my head but she'd already grabbed her books, grinning at Ash, happy to do as the cute new guy asked. She hung around to flirt with him a bit more, but he'd already turned to talk to me. Roxy flopped down in a seat diagonally behind us.

"You disappeared on me yesterday," Ash said, sounding disappointed.

Groan. I tried to tell myself Ash was just a normal guy. Any weirdness was probably coming from him being eager to make friends in a new place. But I didn't need any more complication in my life right now. I wanted things to be as simple as possible.

I brushed some dust off my table and pretended I didn't hear him. Where was Mr. Jones? What was taking him so long?

The classroom was a noisy mix of a dozen different conversations. Half the kids in the class were away from their seats, talking to their friends, sitting on desks, or playing catch with balled up paper.

"You're really strong, you know that?" Ash said.

I spun towards him. What did he know? Had he seen?

He watched me, and there was something more calculating now in that cheery grin of his. His eyes searched mine and I frowned. *Damnit, boy, stop being so suspect!*

"Ash, this is Dean," I deflected. I almost added '*my boyfriend,*' but I didn't know if we were label-ready. "Have you met each other yet?"

Dean waved politely and reached out a hand. Ash met it and they shook hands behind my chair. My heart sank. Making new friends was something Dean really did need. I just wasn't sure if Ash was the best option. I didn't miss the way Ash shivered when he came into contact with Dean. It didn't help me lay to rest my questions and suspicions. Still, I tried to get the two of them talking, mostly so I could avoid Ash, as I flicked more dust off my desk.

What was with the dust?

I looked up to see a small crack in the ceiling above me. A thin stream of dust trickled continuously down to my desk like a gossamer waterfall.

I pushed my chair back slowly, staring at the crumbs of ceiling hitting my desk. My heart thumped.

A letter-sized piece of plasterboard crashed down onto my desk loud enough to shut the whole room up.

Then the whole roof came down.

Fear crashed into me like a tsunami. Dean had either stopped blocking out of shock, or the sheer quantity of terror was enough to turn on my powers in a big way even with him nearby.

Pain shot through me, and I winced, fighting against it. I

had to act, but had maybe only seconds before the level of emotions I was absorbing would be too much.

Time seemed to slow to a crawl, but it was really me, moving faster, thinking faster, seeing faster. *I could make these seconds count.*

The roof was collapsing right into the center of the room. Dean, Ash, Roxy, four other kids and me were directly underneath it.

I shoved the chair out from under me, jumping to my feet. I kicked out, hard, at the desk in line with the students in danger. One, two, three were caught up in a tangle as desk-hit-student-hit-chair-hit-desk, skidding them across the room. Probably bruising and winding them too. *Better than the alternative.*

Movement flickered in the corner of my eye and I saw Roxy, Ash, and one other boy were safe under the teacher's sturdier desk.

The rest of the class had made it to the edges of the room, shielding their heads with their arms from the smaller debris.

There were just Dean and I left. I gritted my teeth, trying to stay focused. *Dean.* My heart pounded his name as my eyes searched for him through the growing cloud of dust and greenness of fear overwhelming my system.

Dean moved in slow motion, reaching out to me. I reached out to him in return and sped the two of us into a corner. Our bodies pressed together, as though we were each trying to be a human-shield for the other. His blocking power returned. I gasped in relief as the empathic intensity lessened and time returned to normal speed.

The ceiling that had seemed to hover for those few split seconds crashed down like thunder. Plasterboard, concrete, and roof tiles hurtled down all around us.

I hope no one was left under there. Clouds of dust rose as the sound of falling debris softened into a rain-like patter.

Mr. Jones appeared in the doorway. "What on earth? Is everyone okay?"

I could see him do a headcount around the room and I followed his gaze, counting as well. Chalky dust hung in the air, making it hard to see, but everyone was clear. A few students cradled sore spots on heads and waists where either the debris or the sliding desks had hit them. A couple of kids were crying.

The largest slab of roof that came down heavy lay flat on the floor with nothing under it, no human pancakes in sight. *I did that,* I thought proudly. *I saved us.*

"Out," Mr. Jones yelled. "Calm and quick. Leave your bags." He split his attention between ushering the class out of the room and yelling down the hall for another teacher to call in emergency services.

Our class had just made it outside when we heard sirens. Ambulance, police, and an emergency rescue vehicle showed up within moments of each other. We were all giddy. The shock and adrenaline of the event—and the lack of serious casualties—turned into teenage excitement, and everyone was gossiping and recounting their version of events.

EMTs began triaging kids, dealing with those who'd taken something to the head first. Some were given oxygen to help with their breathing.

Dean had a small gash on his forearm, and was taken into an ambulance to get it cleaned and dressed. I hoped he'd get them to have a quick look at his wound site too, in case he'd strained it. I tried to go with him, but had already been checked over and given the all clear, and had to remain away from the medical workers.

I recognized Terry, mingling around and checking up on everything. It didn't make much sense for him to be there now he was a detective, but he always was very 'community minded,' as Dad would say. He saw me too and waved. I wiggled my fingers and smiled awkwardly in return, not really wanting everyone here to see I was friends with a cop. I turned my attention to my phone so it seemed I was busy, and there was a text there from Nati.

Nati: OMGGGGGGGGGEE gurl! You OK? They won't let us in that part of the school. Kids saying the whole building is flat *Crying*

I typed out a quick reply, reassuring her everyone was all right.

When I looked up, Terry was there anyway.

"Hi, Detective Pence," I said, as politely as I could.

He smiled and brushed at some dust on his uniform where a kid must have bumped against him. "Olivia. So glad you're okay. Especially after how upset your parents were due to your last little adventure." He grinned perfect teeth at me as though we were co-conspirators and he wasn't just rubbing salt into my guilt. He always put on the buddy-cop performance though, and with his sparkling eyes, blond hair and million-dollar smile, sometimes he sold it.

"It seems as though the earthquake damaged parts of the school's roof—more than anyone realized," he started explaining to me as I fidgeted on the spot, hoping he'd move on. "Really lucky there were no serious injuries. Really lucky."

"Yeah. Lucky." My mind raced. I hoped what I did back in the room hadn't been too obvious, too visible to everyone in the class. Did they see me kick out and push the desks? Was I moving fast enough to be unnoticeable, or just fast enough to look like I was moving weirdly fast? One kid who had been right beside me was walking with a limp. It must have been from where the desk hit him. He didn't seem to be paying me any attention, and just seemed happy and no doubt shocked that he wasn't under a pile of rubble right now.

And then there was Ash.

I looked around the covered learning area where we'd evacuated to and spotted Roxy talking to another police officer. She was gesturing wildly about what had happened, and saw her point at Ash. I frowned. I'd seen something move fast in the room. At a time when everything normal seemed to be going in slow motion.

Ash was making a phone call and then turned to leave. I wasn't sure if any of us were supposed to be going yet. But part of me was glad he wasn't sticking around for questioning as I wondered again what his deal was.

"Yeah. I don't know what happened," I said, covering for myself and maybe Ash as well. "We were all just really lucky."

Terry nodded, flashed his grin again, and moved on to talk to some teachers.

"Hey," Dean said from behind me. I turned and almost threw myself into his arms, until I saw the bandage wrapping one of them.

"You okay?" I asked instead, putting my hands in my pockets

and hoping I hadn't leaned too awkwardly close to Dean.

"Fine. Was just worried about you. But you saved all of us." Dean's voice was low, just for me. He held my gaze intensely, and gave me a single nod.

"I, ah, I don't think it was me only."

Dean looked across to the school gates, dropping his voice even more. "Maybe, yeah. You think Ash is an empath?"

"*For sure* an empath!" I whispered back, relieved to be on the same page.

"What does that mean? Trouble?"

I opened my mouth, but didn't have an answer. Ash wasn't just displaying a reaction to Dean's presence. He'd *used* his powers. Maybe it was just on instinct, the very first time they had kicked in for him. It didn't seem that way to me, though. And while he seemed nice and friendly, I'd been tricked by people masking their true selves before.

"I don't know," I said. "We'll just have to wait and see, and be ready."

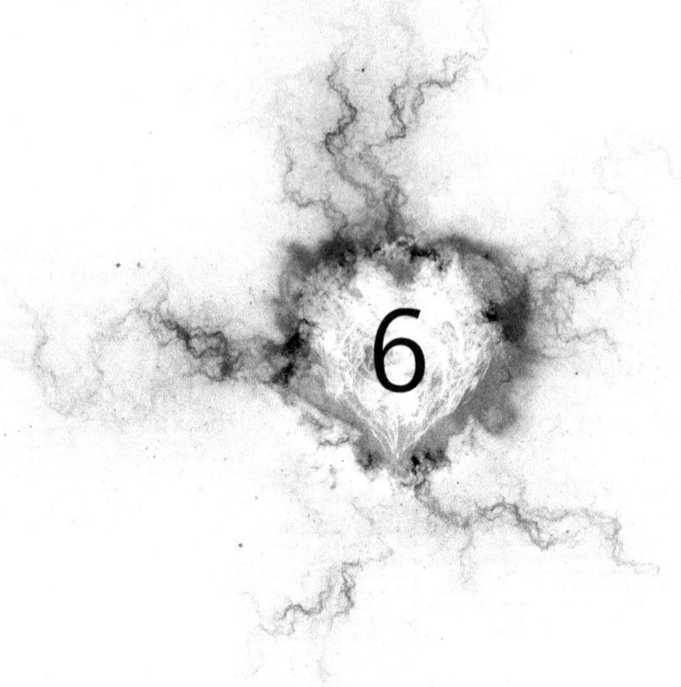

6

Dean took off his motorbike helmet. "You keep on making me break your parents' rules."

I could hardly hear him through the helmet I wore. My hands were still on his hips from the ride and we'd just pulled up into the parking lot outside of The Bellscroft Mental Healthcare Facility. Or as I called it, *The Asylum*.

The psychologist we were meant to be seeing did counselling out of an office here and the whole thing just made me feel even more like my parents really did think I was insane. Even though they kept referring to her as a counsellor, and our visits as counselling, I had visions of electro-shock therapy in my future.

"Don't worry, they won't find out," I bluffed, worrying that my parents always seemed to have ways of knowing, like they could read my mind. Or maybe I was just never as covert as I thought I was.

I pushed at my helmet, the snug fit making it feel like my head was going to pop off along with it. Dean hopped off the bike and helped me. I shook out my hair and smiled. It had been a fun ride, and a good excuse to lean into Dean and feel his warmth as we rode down through town. My parents had wanted to take us to our first meeting, but it was straight after school and they were working, so I said we'd catch the bus directly to the appointment. Then we conveniently forgot until we were back at home, and with no busses scheduled for another half hour, Dean's bike seemed like a better option than being late to our first appointment. I didn't want it to seem like we were avoiding going. I was sure that would be a psychologically red flag.

The grounds of the facility were nice, and not at all creepy or foreboding like I'd imagined. Set on a large block downtown, there were high fences, but inside neat gardens surrounded an art-deco era mansion that, despite being old, was more welcoming than spooky.

"Ready?" Dean asked.

"As I'll ever be. You?"

He nodded, eyes on the building.

Both of us had been shaken up by the roof collapse at school. On its own, it didn't seem like a huge event compared to what else we'd been through, but it was a bit like the straw on the camel's massive pile of trauma.

I spent most of the night afterwards in my comfiest clothes, eating crisps dipped in ice cream, and alternating between hugs with my teary, relieved parents and snuggles on the couch with Dean. I had nuzzled up next to him and he'd, somewhat stiffly, put his arm around me. In some ways, he seemed more distant, colder than he had been when we'd first met, but I was starting to understand that that was how he dealt with things like this. Things like *yet another near miss of losing someone he loved.*

That thought alone warmed me—maybe I was someone he loved. I had planted one kiss on his shoulder, then let him be as we'd watched cartoons together.

That was a week ago, and I knew in some ways we were both looking forward to having a chat with a counsellor. The trauma was real. But I also had no idea what to expect. Would it be like on TV shows? Would she ask me, 'How does that make you feel?' a lot? I guessed I was about to find out.

A pleasant woman with wiry black hair directed us from the front desk, down a corridor to where we'd find the waiting room. On the way, I couldn't help but snoop, arching my neck and peering down side corridors or into rooms, curious about what really happened in places like this. It all seemed very normal, a bit like a regular hospital, but there were less outward signs of illness—less IV stands and bandages, and more comfy chairs and social areas. The people were mostly calm, and seemed content, if quiet. We passed an elderly man with hollow, glazed eyes being helped down the corridor by a nurse, and a shiver ran down my spine.

"Is it cold in here?" I asked Dean.

"Not really."

I glanced back at the old man and frowned. He had an identification tag with what looked like medical care notes clipped to his chest, but all I could read was *Holbrook*.

We reached the waiting room and I was called in right away. Dean gave me a searching look and a small nod, which I returned, adding a half-smile.

The counsellor said, "Call me Debbie," and welcomed me into her office.

She was a tiny woman with a sweet face made quirky by eyes that were slightly too close together. She gestured to one of the two simple office chairs in the room and took a seat. Beside me was a glass of water and a box of tissues. Certificates hung on the walls, books on psychology filled shelves around the room, and a few baskets of toys sat in the corner, probably for her younger patients.

The session was … interesting. Debbie got me talking, just prompting me to chat through everything that had happened. I stuck to the mundane details and left out anything beyond normal. I did tell her that there were things that had happened that seemed … *strange*, that I couldn't explain, as backup for the likely case my story didn't add up. I thought that would be when she started scribbling secret notes about my sanity, but she said it was to be expected. Trauma could often leave people confused about what was real and what they experienced, make them seek fantasy excuses for terrible events.

Even with Dean just out in the waiting room, I was still picking up a lot of emotions in the building. It made me twitchy and I rambled. Debbie just listened, sometimes asking me to explain a bit more or giving me a moment to think about *how it made me feel*. I wasn't sure how that was going to help me, but I thought it did. I even used the tissues, twice. The session was a lot like on TV and also not. And it was over before I knew it.

I tag-teamed Dean, and as he walked in and closed the door, part of me wished I could hear what he would say. How much would he open up? Would he reveal more to Debbie than he did to me? Would he simply state the facts or would he let some emotion break free?

My strange counsellor-related jealousy was banished by a commotion down the hallway. It was the first sign of trouble I'd seen since we arrived, the sort of cliché I was expecting from a horror-style institution. Three very flustered nurses were struggling to subdue a small boy—or was it a girl? Someone petite and blond and from this distance, very non-binary.

Red emotion swirled around all of them. The heat of the nurse's anger reached me and my muscles tensed and grew strong. I felt like I could punch a hole in the wall, and part of me wanted to, just to release the tension of all this power.

The kid was given an injection of some kind, calmed quickly, then was ushered away. How did one small person need three big men to hold them down? I was worried that I knew exactly how.

By feeling the way anger just made me feel.

I was on my feet, but they were already gone. I couldn't risk following or I'd get too far away from Dean.

I sat down again, my heart racing. Was that kid an empath?

And the old man before who gave me chills ... was he a blocker? Or was I looking for paranormal answers to regular events? Was I seeing empaths everywhere, in Ash, in the people here? Maybe the kid was an addict in a drug-fueled rage. Maybe I just felt cold. It could all be nothing.

But I couldn't get past the worries. If no one had explained my empath powers to me, how sane would I feel right now?

My thoughts were still spinning when Dean's session finished and he came out. His eyes seemed red around the edges and I wanted to hug him, but instead just stood close enough that our hands touched.

We both thanked Debbie and made our way to the exit. I bumped my snooping up a notch, but didn't see anything else suspicious.

"I think I saw an empath in there," I told Dean almost bashfully when we reached his bike.

He looked thoughtful for a moment. "You think they don't know what they are?"

He understood right away, which made me even more certain I was on the right track. "If we didn't know what we were, what was happening with our bodies and emotions, I think I might be a permanent resident in there too."

"What can we do?" Dean asked.

I groaned. "I don't know. I'm not even sure it is what I think it is. I guess we wait and watch again. Maybe next time we can try and talk to them, if that's allowed. I get the feeling the rules might be strict about that sort of thing." I felt hopeless. I wanted to help, but didn't even know where to start. This seemed so much bigger than pushing some kids out from under a falling ceiling.

We'd taken the wait-and-see approach with Ash, but hadn't even seen him again since naming our suspicions. Which was odd in itself, unless he also hadn't known what he was, and was gone because he wasn't coping with the experience of finding out about his powers. I pouted like a very sad clown.

"You'll work something out." Dean handed me my helmet. "Since we're breaking rules anyway, I think I know what might cheer you up. Something I know you enjoy."

"What?" I asked, my fingers lingering on his as I took the helmet from him.

"Flying." Dean put his helmet on and swung his leg over the bike. He slid to the back of the seat, and patted the spot in front of him. "I'll show you how."

My grin in return was massive and mischievous.

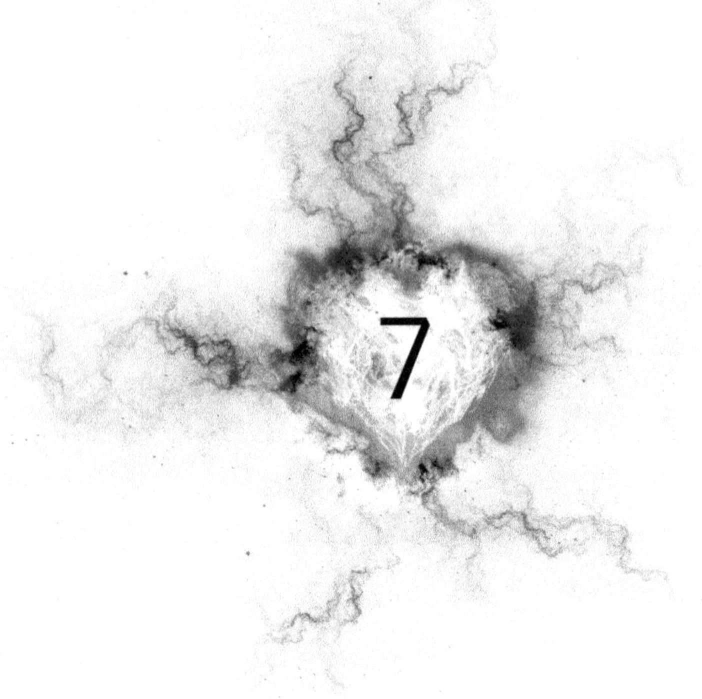

7

School took a while to return to normal after the ceiling collapse.

Everyone wanted the full story from those of us in the room, and rumors had spread about Ash, who hadn't returned to school since. Mostly from Roxy, who was obviously pining for him. She believed he was the one who saved everyone's lives through some kind of martial arts prowess, which I thought seemed like stereotyping.

But maybe I was stereotyping by thinking he could also be an empath. Him and the people at the institute. I felt like I was seeing empaths everywhere and I doubted they'd be that common.

Maybe it was like Debbie said—I was seeing the paranormal in the normal because of the trauma I'd been through.

Nati, Dean, and I had a free period at the end of the day and even though we spent most of it in study room, we still ended up down at the bus stop before any supervising teachers or most of the other students. Nati normally drove home since she owned her own car, but that car was a beat-up relic which frequently found itself at the mechanics to stay roadworthy. I was quietly grateful for more time with her.

Dean had been holding my hand since we left class. A detail neither I nor Nati found small. I wondered if the counselling had anything to do with this huge-for-Dean public display of affection. Nati found it squee-worthy and practically skipped around us as we waited at the school gates, like she was about to break into the K-I-S-S-I-N-G song any moment.

"I can cover for you guys if you want some alone time. I am an awesome lookout for make-out-stopping interruptions."

Dean's hand tensed, and I remembered our last attempt at making out. "Thanks, Nati. We're okay for now."

Nati gave me a look up and down, then gave Dean a look up and down. "Oh hi, hot teenage girl. Oh hi, hot teenage boy. How are you two not smushed together twenty-four-seven? This sexual tension is driving me insane and I'm just a bystander."

Yeah, I knew how she felt. Where Dean's hand sat in mine, the gentle pressure of his fingers around mine, it seemed to set my whole body on fire. I wanted more, and I knew I couldn't have it.

"Nati, I love you, but seriously, just drop it, okay? There's other stuff going on than just … just drop it."

As if I'd been talking to him, Dean let go of my hand.

Nati frowned, realizing she'd gone too far. She pouted, widened her arms into a hug position, and baby-stepped toward me.

I accepted her silent apology and hugged her back.

She let go then turned to Dean, her pout now cheeky. "You get one too!"

Dean had no chance of escape as Nati wrapped around him. Dean begrudgingly accepted her hug, and even patted her awkwardly on the back.

I was chuckling quietly at them when I heard a vehicle pull up behind me and the sliding sound of a van door.

Hands grabbed at me, locking around my arms.

I was dragged off my feet. Nati and Dean broke their hug, shock all over their faces. Two figures in black SWAT-team-style outfits dragged me toward a gray van. *I told you so!* My brain announced with ironic triumph, over my fear.

The surprise dropped Dean's blocking away, and I was hit

with a wall of energy as he no longer subdued my rampant powers.

"Livvy!" Dean and Nati yelled in unison.

Dean tried to get to me and one of my assailants knocked him flat onto the concrete. "Dean!" I screamed, furious they'd hurt him. I tried to fight back, but the attackers were strong. *Super* strong. I was hefted and thrown into the back of the van. I landed with a thud. The door closed.

I screamed, lashing out at the door, trying to pull it open. I cracked the interior panel with my fist and felt the metal bend underneath my pressure. The engine rumbled, and I was thrown to the side as we sped away. Away from Dean, way too fast.

My vision blurred with streams of colorful energy, emotional auras and power rushing into me unchecked. I turned to the closest threat and threw a punch. They blocked with their forearm and I felt it crack. The van spun around a corner and my next hit missed. My mind buzzed, swirled, faded.

I cried out as the waves of emotion became too much. I flailed, fighting the air. The attackers grabbed at me again, two, maybe three of them working together, and I was pinned facedown, just in time for the seizure to hit.

Darkness took me.

I gasped back into consciousness. My head ached, but was clear. My mouth tasted of blood.

I was … lying on a mattress? In a weird, sterile space. It was an odd room, like an office or meeting room, but set up with a simple metal-framed bed, basic kitchenette, and a table and chairs. My hands weren't bound in any way, and I reached straight for my pocket, where my phone should have been, and found it gone.

Ash sat on the table, his feet on one of the chairs, hands clasped over his knees, watching me.

I sat up slowly. A low level of energy hummed inside me, but I could sense almost no anger or fear or any strong emotion nearby. It was as though Ash was the only person for hundreds of feet around, and he was eerily calm.

I wasn't.

"Ash? WHAT THE ACTUAL FLEEP?" I rubbed my forehead where a small bump had risen. "Did you get kidnapped too? Who were those guys?"

"Hey Livvy," he said, like we were best friends. He smiled his cheery grin, but the calculation in his eyes remained. "Time we had a proper talk."

"A *talk*? You … did you do this? Did you seriously just have me kidnapped to have a talk?" I couldn't make sense of why

I was here, and why Ash was here, or where *here* was. There were no windows or clues as to our location. *What in blue-blaze-balls is going on?*

"Since you found out I'm a proesthian too, there's no point trying to hide it. Not for either one of us."

My confusion made me squint. "A pro-what?"

Ash frowned very slightly. "A proesthian."

I stared blankly.

"A primal?" he tried again.

I blinked, continued staring, frowned.

"An empath?"

"Oh," I said, before realizing maybe I shouldn't give him confirmation I understood even that much.

"There we go." Ash hopped down off the table and walked up in front of me. "You don't seem to know much about empaths. But you like them, don't you?"

My hands became fists. Did he mean Dean? Did they, whoever *they* were, kidnap Dean too? He must be here somewhere, otherwise I'd still be a twitching drooling mess. Was he in another room nearby?

I swung my legs off the bed and stood face-to-face with Ash. He suddenly seemed older, smarter, than he ever did at school. He squared his shoulders to mine.

"Where is Dean? Did you and your mercs kidnap him, too?"

"Why would we—?" Ash frowned, and rubbed his temples. "Look, I'm sorry about how we had to get you here. But I needed to be alone with you, and you were never alone. But now we are, just you and me. You know I'm like you. Isn't there … anything you want from me?"

SERIOUSLY? The word flashed in my mind in giant neon letters. "Even not counting the abduction, I'm really not interested in you in that way."

Ash half sighed, half chuckled. "I didn't mean …"

What else could he mean? "Oh, like information or training or something? Is this some kind of weird superpower hazing thing? You need to quit with the cryptic because I'm just not getting onboard here."

Ash's shoulders dropped. He must have been tense. His whole body had been on guard. From me?

He turned and looked up into the corner of the room. I followed his gaze and noticed a camera. He talked directly to it. "My assessment stands. I don't think we've got the right one. She seems completely clueless."

"Insult me like I'm not standing right here. Why not?" I muttered.

A loud, mechanical unlocking sound came from the door and

it opened. A man and woman wearing suits came in, both pale-skinned and grim-faced. Weirdly, they were followed by an Asian girl who looked about twelve years old and far too colorful for the situation. Before they closed the door, I saw a glimpse of half a dozen adults in the SWAT-style uniforms in the hall outside. They looked as if they were ready to make a move, and yet also somehow really calm. So much for it being just Ash and me. And so weird that I couldn't sense their emotions.

The woman held a tablet device which showed the camera-angle view of the room we were in. She swiped it closed only after I'd seen it, as though she wanted me to know they'd been watching.

I looked carefully at her and the man.

I knew them. I'd seen them before. I raced through my memory, trying to work out where I knew their faces, and it pinged. They were the couple from the hospital who I saw looking over Jake, Donny, and Jamie.

My confusion levels were epic, and fear also started to shake me up. What had I gotten myself into? Myself and Dean? This was some serious shady organization stuff.

I giggled nervously. "Is this the part where you give me some answers, or the part where you make me disappear?"

The woman gave me a chilling look. "Take a seat."

I dropped into a chair like an obedient puppy. The older

couple sat down across from me and Ash and the girl stood behind them. The girl seemed super calm. Not calm in the nearly robotic way Dean seemed sometimes, but in a really chilled and contented way that made me feel good inside too. Her My Little Pony multi-colored pastel hair and lemon-yellow cardigan also made me happy.

But If I knew only one thing, I knew I was dealing with empaths here. Ash definitely—the guys in the van, probably. The girl, maybe. What kind of empaths, I wasn't sure, now there were empaths and blockers and pro-whatsies on the table apparently too.

I couldn't trust my feelings. I had to stay alert. I hadn't been restrained or bound in any way, but the door had made a locking sound again when it closed. I didn't know if I was some kind of prisoner, or if I'd be free to get up and leave. The SWAT guys could still be outside, and I wasn't sure I could take them all on. My powers felt weird. Different to when Dean was keeping them subdued. More low-level, like there was nothing around to draw from rather than actually being turned off.

So for now I would sit and see what these people had to say.

"You can call me Dr. Crossman," the woman said. With her pin-up hair style and lazily beautiful face, she looked like she'd just walked out of a detective noir movie. What kind of doctor was she? "And this is Mr. Crossman," she said, gesturing to the man.

I confirmed wedding rings on both of them. I thought they gave off a couple sort of vibe, a bit like Bonny and Clyde might.

Mr. Crossman had a clean-cut boy-scout type appearance, thick black hair, and a sparkle in his eye that didn't seem wholesome and boy-scout like at all. "You've probably worked out by now that Ash was placed in your classes to observe you. His empath powers were revealed during the roof-collapse incident so we had to pull him from the mission, but we weren't finished assessing your risk. That's why we decided to bring you in."

Beyond Ash being an empath, I hadn't worked anything out. But I liked that they thought so highly of my deductive abilities. "And have you finished assessing my *risk* now?"

Dr. Crossman held my gaze in a way that unnerved me. "We're hunting for an empath who has been stealing power from others."

My chest grew tight. They must know what I did to Jake, Jamie, and Donny. *That's why I'm here. For ... punishment?*

I rambled. "I'm not, I mean, I didn't mean to. I didn't want to steal anything." Panic made my vision swim. I jerked to my feet; my chair fell back. But the door was locked, I was surrounded, there was no window, no escape.

The girl moved quickly to me and put a hand on my arm and one on my face, turning it toward her. "Shh, it's okay."

"Careful, Rayni," Ash said, following her to my side. They had matching accents.

"We're okay, aren't we?" Rayni smiled up at me. Golden-yellow contentment and calm swirled around her and washed over me. It pushed into me so forcefully that it seemed to force out all other emotions, like a rainbow cloud leaving me.

The panic faded. I could feel my emotions dulling, my adrenaline wearing off. I tried to fight it, to stay in charge of how I felt, but the calm pushed back harder. Ash righted my chair, and I drifted back down into it.

"She's a strong one." Rayni seemed out of breath, and stayed at my side, one hand on my arm. This was nice. She was nice. Everything was okay. *Golden.* My eyelids drooped half-closed.

"Thanks, Rayni," Dr. Crossman said. "As I was saying, we are trying to track down an empath who is hurting other empaths, taking their powers. We wanted to test you by giving you a situation that, if you were our target, you couldn't resist."

In my calm came a sort of clarity. "You used Ash for bait? Was he trying to get me to drain him?"

"He was perfectly safe; we were monitoring the whole thing."

I remembered the camera and the men outside, and nodded as though it made perfect sense. I could feel the small pressure in the pit of my gut from my emotions silently screaming. "But Ash said I'm not the one?"

"You clearly didn't have any idea what was going on," Ash confirmed.

"But you have drained empaths before," Dr. Crossman said coldly.

I nodded, and my eyelids started to slip closed. My breathing was short and shallow, like my body had decided it wasn't necessary anymore. Everything was okay.

Ash grabbed my shoulder before I faceplanted on the desk. "Rayni, ease up a bit."

"Omigod, I'm so sorry! She's just so strong. I haven't pushed that hard before."

My emotions eased back under my own control. The fear and panic and worry, the confusion and disgust that these adults had used Ash as bait, all became my own again. Followed by the anger that they were holding me here, that they'd kidnapped me, and that I didn't know what they would do to me next.

"What are you doing to me?" I wanted to cry.

Rayni looked genuinely upset, flushing a sickly aqua-blue aura, her lips quivering. She looked entirely like the child she was. She quickly got her emotions under control again and returned to a calm state. But whatever she'd done a moment ago she wasn't doing anymore, not to the same levels. I wasn't being smothered.

"Rayni is here because of your reaction to us acquiring you." Mr. Crossman said.

"Kidnapping me," I muttered.

"We know absorbing additional powers can result in heightened emotions and unstable behavior. Rayni's emogen ability is helping to keep you level, and keeping those around us level so you aren't drawing in too much. Frankly, we're amazed you've done so well on your own so far."

Every answer they gave raised a dozen new questions and I wasn't keeping up. So Dean wasn't here somewhere? Did they not know about him? Rayni was the one keeping me from frothing on the floor? What in empath-land was an emogen?

I didn't have time to ask anything before Mr. Crossman picked up the tablet device and opened a screen showing footage from the bank shooting. He swiped across and there was a police report from the fireman I saved. He swiped again, and kept swiping, and there were photos of the park marked out with crime-scene tape and evidence flags, and a video of Jamie, Jake, and Donny in hospital beds. And then, a surveillance camera view of the park. That night, with me fighting the others, tearing their emotions from their bodies. I could see Dean lying still in the foreground of the video. I watched with my mouth open and tears started running down my cheeks. There was no visual sign on the video of the emotions leaving them, no glow or aura the camera could see, but the moment was clear. One by one, they dropped to the ground.

"How did you get that? Why don't the police—why don't they know?" My voice was hushed with guilt and sadness.

"We made sure this video disappeared before the police could get it."

They covered it up. These people, this organization, whatever it was—they hid evidence. And what else? Detective Phillips seemed to give up on me so easily, and after the bank, none of what happened had made the news. *That was just the sort of manipulation organized empaths could perform.*

Dr. Crossman softened a little. "The video always seemed to tell the story of a girl fighting for self-defense. And then things went too far. We've known of the criminal actions of this group for some time, and it's clear you got caught up in it and were only with them briefly. But still, we wanted to be sure that what we saw was true. Sometimes images lie. Maybe you were the one infiltrating their group, manipulating their actions in order to steal their powers."

I shook my head and a tear splattered on the table. The Crossmans clearly knew everything. There was no point denying what I'd done. But they didn't seem to know anything about Dean, so I made sure to keep him out of it. "I didn't mean to do it. I didn't even know what I was doing. I'd only known about empaths for barely a week, and I know nothing about emogens or proessie-thingies or any of this. I don't even know how I took from them what I did. I'd give it all back if I could. I'd do anything to give it back."

Dr. Crossman gave me a piercing look. "I hope you really mean that. Come with me. I need to show you something." She stood up from the table, and that seemed to signal everyone else in the room to move as well.

The Crossmans left the room first and I followed after them, with Ash and Rayni behind me. As we headed out into the corridor, the people on guard there separated to let us through, and then followed along behind as well. *Guess I'm still not entirely trusted yet.*

Wherever they were taking me, they were taking me there silently. The halls we walked down were plain, like they belonged to an office building or budget motel, and all doors were closed, so I couldn't sticky beak. We reached an elevator and, based on the internal buttons, this building was a decent size, taller than any in Bellscroft. We were on the sixth floor of ten.

Mr. Crossman pressed the button for the first floor, and addressed the SWAT team. "We should be fine from here."

I eyed him and wondered what type of empath he was, now I knew that empaths had types. With Rayni keeping my emotional levels subdued, I wasn't sure I'd be able to beat even her and Ash if it came to a violent getaway, let alone two expert adult empaths of whatever type the Crossmans were.

The elevator opened up to another plain hallway and we headed off to the right. Mr. Crossman stopped at a double door and swung one open, letting Dr. Crossman then myself through first. I held my breath, waiting to see where they had led me. I half expected it would be my prison cell.

Instead, I saw what looked like an intensive care ward.

A dozen hospital beds were laid out next to each other. On seven of the beds lay lifeless bodies.

Machines hummed along near each patient, reading vital signs and providing nutrients through feeding tubes. Half hidden behind a partition curtain, a nurse worked on massaging and exercising one of the patient's legs. He saw us come in, nodded to Dr. Crossman, then left us in privacy.

"What is this place?" I whispered. "Who are these—?"

People, I was about to ask, then I saw the beautiful face of the body closest to me. *Jake.* His re-growth-streaked blond hair lay greasy and flat against his head.

My eyes darted around, confirming my suspicions. *Jamie. Donny.* They were all there. My heart pounded, flighty, like a scared rabbit.

Something rubbed past my leg and I jumped nearly three feet into the air.

"Mew." A black and white cat circled us, as though greeting me, Ash, Rayni and the Crossmans.

No one else seemed confused or surprised by the cat. *Oookay.*

Dr. Crossman, who until now had been so composed I hadn't seen a hint of color on her, started to show wisps of blue sadness. "These are the three empaths you drained. And four more, drained by someone else."

That was why the Crossmans were at the hospital. They must have gone there to collect the three of them, to bring them here.

"Each of the other four were found one at a time. When you drained these three all at once, it didn't fit the pattern, but we had to be sure. Finding the leech is our biggest priority."

"There's someone out there with four other empath's powers?" My voice cracked. How were they even functioning? I couldn't say too much about my own case without letting on about Dean, but I had so many questions.

"At least four. There have been a couple of other empath disappearances where we couldn't locate and confirm the cause. But we are sure the leech is actively hunting and absorbing other empaths' powers."

I glanced at Ash, no longer cheery, and Rayni, so young beside me, and shivered. "What can I do?"

"We want you to try and restore the empaths you have drained. If it can be proven possible, there is hope for the other four as well. If we can discover the identity of the leech and capture them."

"Do you think it's possible?" If it was, then all the intensity would stop. I could be myself again. I could be with Dean. I was hopeful, but I was also still ticked off at the whole kidnapping thing. These people had hurt me, and there was no telling what they would do in the future. What would they do if I simply wasn't able to do what they asked? "I really know nothing about what happened. I didn't even know what type of empath I was before today, or that there were other types."

"There's a lot you don't know," Mr. Crossman said. "If you agree to help, we can train you, teach you everything. Maybe we can find a solution."

"What about you? I mean, you're obviously the expert empaths here. Why can't you try and do something?"

Dr. Crossman and Mr. Crossman both stiffened. I knew I'd said the wrong thing, but I had no idea what it was. She stood beside Jamie's bed, and her hand rested on the mattress near his shoulder. The blue aura of sadness around her intensified and flowed towards me. It almost buckled my knees and I bit back a sob. Rayni also winced, noticing my reaction, and Dr. Crossman's aura dulled.

"We're doing all we can." Mr. Crossman reached into his pocket and pulled my phone out, then handed it back to me. A quick glance at the screen showed it had only been about two hours since I was kidnapped, but there were dozens of missed calls and texts from my parents, Dean, and Nati.

"Will you help us?" Dr. Crossman asked.

Rebellion roiled in me. *Why should I help these people who kidnapped me?* A tear rolled down my cheek, thinking of the worry my parents, Dean, and Nati must be feeling for me right now, but also something else. Even with Rayni using her powers to dull the emotions, I could tell Dr. Crossman was intensely sad. The same kind of sadness only caused by losing someone you love. Regardless of what she'd done, I wanted to help her.

"I'll try. But I'm not the only one you need to win over," I said, and met Dr. Crossman's gaze. "If you want me on your team, kidnapping me wasn't the way to go about it. My parents are going to be pissed."

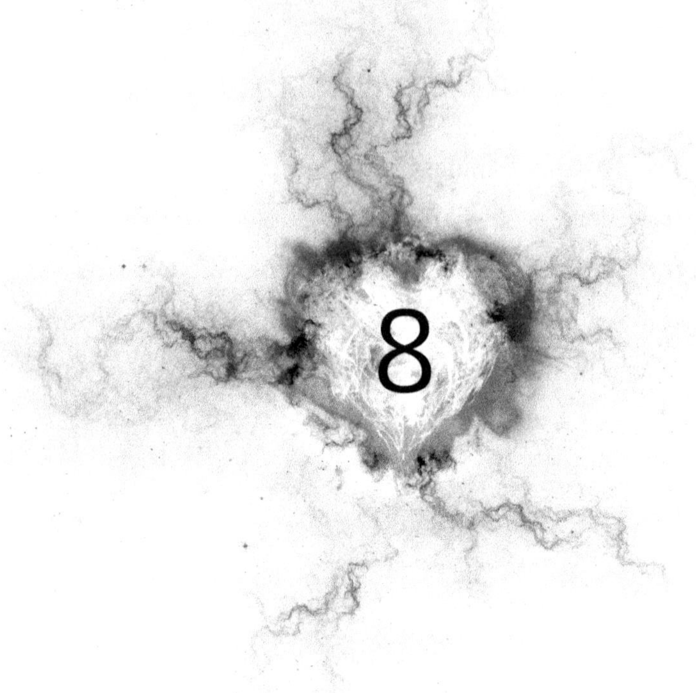

8

I stood at my front door, flanked by the Crossmans. The sun was just starting to set and the flowering lavender in the herb garden swayed in a slight breeze. It was nice to be home. Kidnapped and back before dinner—Limbus were efficient.

Rayni had to come along as well when it had become clear I wasn't coping without her emotion-controlling presence. Ash had apologized for the whole ordeal, and remained behind. I didn't blame him.

It only took one knock on the door for it to burst open, and Mom, who opened it, to burst into tears.

Dad was right behind her, and on the phone. "Terry, she's

home. No. No. Look, I'll call you back," he said.

Dean and Nati spilled out of the house after my parents.

Mom held me. She shook, and swaths of blue sadness flowed off her, replaced with orange and green tones. Relieved, but still worried, almost angry. The colors surrounded us like a blanket.

Nati soon joined in the hug, squeezing past Dad to get in first. "Omigod, that was like something from a movie but it really happened. Did it really happen? Omigod, I don't know how to process this," she said, all in one breath.

Dean stood to the back, still and calm, but something intense filled his eyes. I sighed, happy to be within his blocking aura again. I was worried one of the other empaths would react to his presence, but the Crossmans didn't seem to notice anything. Only Rayni looked a little confused.

A flurry of questions and emotions hit me next. Was I okay? Did they hurt me? Did we need to call the police?

"Yes. No. *No*," I answered as quickly as I could in the short pauses between conversation.

Mom looked warily from me to the Crossmans. "Who are these people? Police? Did they rescue you?"

"Um. No. They're actually the kidnappers." I held my hands up in a pleading 'just hear me out' gesture. "But it's okay. It was sort of a mix-up. They're okay, but we need to have a talk."

"A mix-up? They abducted a child! Broad daylight abduction!" Dad roared.

I held up my pleading hands a bit higher. "They'll explain everything. And you can always call Terry on them if you decide you aren't happy with their explanation." Not that it would do much good, considering how they'd swept evidence of my last adventure away so efficiently.

I reached over and took Nati's hand, squeezing it. "I'll have to tell you all about it later, okay? You should get home; your parents are probably worried too."

She looked teary and overwhelmed. "Only if you think, if you really ..."

"Yeah, it's all good. I'm fine." I smiled my best smile.

"Our driver could give you a ride if you like," Mr. Crossman offered.

"Hells no am I getting a lift with kidnappers! I'll catch the bus, thanks." And after one more tight hug, she was gone.

"Rayni, I'm okay now that I'm home. Feeling much more relaxed. You can take a break. Maybe you can wait in the car?" I suggested, getting concerned she was going to pick Dean as a blocker. She shook her head slightly, as though trying to clear it. Poor thing. She was so young to be involved in this.

She looked to the Crossmans for confirmation. They nodded

and she trotted back down the front yard path between my mom's overgrown herb garden.

"What about the boy?" Dr. Crossman asked, realizing all too easily that I was clearing out people I didn't want to hear this conversation.

"It's okay. He already knows all about me. You've seen the videos; you know who he is. You can trust him."

She didn't look convinced, but nodded and stepped closer to my still frowning parents.

"Dr. Crossman. You can call me Lola." She extended her hand to shake, but my parents looked at her as though she was riddled with leprosy.

"Vincent Crossman." At least he was aware enough to not try and shake their hands. "We apologize sincerely for what you've just endured, but we assure you it was necessary. We had to assess your daughter's risk due to a larger threat we're facing. May we come inside and discuss?"

Dad looked to me. "We can make them leave if you want. Just say."

I sighed. "No, it's okay, really. This is important. Let's go in and talk."

We all took seats around the dining table, and the Crossmans caught my parents up on why I was kidnapped. They spoke a lot more officially with them than they had with me. They were from an *organization* called Limbus, and were seeking a *rogue threat* within the *empath community*, and given my recent activities, they had me marked as a *potential suspect*, and circumstances required I be *forcibly acquired for interrogation*. Same stuff. Bigger words.

"Limbus is dedicated to studying, policing, and training empaths." Dr. Crossman leaned toward my parents across the table. "On record, we work as a freelance spy agency for the government, and as far as the government knows, that's all we do. But Limbus has been a secret empath organization for decades."

"*Secret* being the key word here," Mr. Crossman emphasized. "We expect you understand the importance of keeping the existence of empaths hidden, as it directly affects your daughter."

"We do understand. I also understand you wouldn't be telling us all this if you didn't want something from us or Olivia," Mom said, tapping the table with two fingers.

"Besides our silence on the whole kidnapping affair," Dad muttered.

Dr. Crossman's lips grew thin. She hesitated, then continued her spiel as though she hadn't been interrupted. "Limbus has a science and development division, special agent division, and monitoring division. We offer training in all these areas, which will give your daughter a greater understanding of her talents, and also job opportunities in the long run."

"You mean you want her to sign up with you lot? After you kidnapped her?" Dad's tone was incredulous.

Mr. Crossman replied, "We already have a small group of youths in training at our Bellston Main facility. Olivia is familiar with two of them already. Joining them would be of great advantage to her, and it's better for all empaths to be under the Limbus umbrella, especially with current circumstances."

"Which are?" Mom asked tersely. She tapped her fingertips around her cup of tea, which she hadn't taken a sip of yet.

I answered quickly, hoping hearing it from me would get my parents onboard. "Someone's attacking empaths. Another empath, seeking out and stealing their powers."

My parents leaned back in their chairs, as though pushed away by the words. Dad rubbed the bridge of his nose. "Sounds like a good reason to me to *not* be around other empaths right now."

"Dad, they know so much more than me, like about proesthians, and that there are different kinds of empaths." My eyes strayed over to Dean briefly and then back to my parents before my look could betray him. I was still curious why the Crossmans didn't seem to notice him at all. They hadn't mentioned blockers at all yet. Maybe they didn't know. Maybe Dean was focusing all his blocking on me and making sure not to block them? It was something he'd been able to do in the past, but so far, our levelling up of skills had been hit and miss. Maybe training with Limbus would be good for him, too. Still, I didn't want to reveal him just yet. Just in case it didn't go well. And it should be his choice, either way.

I looked down at my fidgeting fingers, unsure even of what choice I wanted to make myself. "There's just ... so much I don't know."

"Do you even understand the core theory of empath powers?" Dr. Crossman asked. Her tone was curious more than mocking, but I still felt embarrassed when I shook my head.

"As our scientists currently understand it, empaths are a subset of human evolution, with far more advanced adrenal and social-neural receptors. We believe empaths evolved to be protectors within human social groups." Dr. Crossman held my gaze. I could tell this was an area she was passionate about, the science side of things. I couldn't help compare her to Jake, and how little he seemed to know about empaths, and how little he cared to know, beyond what the powers could gain him.

Dr. Crossman continued. "Even from the time we lived in

simple tribes, proesthians, like yourself—"

"Primals is the more common term," Mr. Crossman slipped in, like he thought we needed layman's terms.

"*Primals* were always the strongest, fastest warriors in the tribe. Because humans are a community animal, if one member of that community feels scared, it could mean there is danger to be scared of. In that case, being able to move the fastest is a great benefit and could save your life and the lives of others. If there is anger in the community, it's a warlike emotion, and the need to be able to fight might be important, so strength is increased. It's like a super-heightened fight-or-flight response. Primals have the ability to turn the very emotions of the community around them into what they need to protect that group."

"What about happiness? Love?" I asked, reminded of my conversation with Emma when she scoffed at the idea. How would Dr. Crossman respond?

"Happy emotions don't have as much direct physical effect, since a happy tribe doesn't generally signify the presence of a fight-or-flight situation," she said.

I wanted to argue that love had been the emotion that gave me my greatest strength. That beyond fight-or-flight, love was the emotion needed to give you the desire to protect your tribe, and the power.

But I said nothing. They clearly knew a lot more than me about the science side of it all. I knew I wasn't wrong, but I knew there was so much I still needed to learn. The idea of learning with them gave me mixed feelings.

"You seem to know your stuff," Dad said.

"I've worked hard to do so," Dr. Crossman replied.

Mom finally sipped her tea, then placed the mug down heavily on the table. "I think that's enough for now." Everyone turned to her. "We'll talk about this with Livvy, but right now, I'd like you to leave my house. If Livvy does become involved in Limbus, expect her to come along with a formal complaint about your actions today."

Dad stood up to see them out, the threat in his tone clear. "And that's a really big *if*."

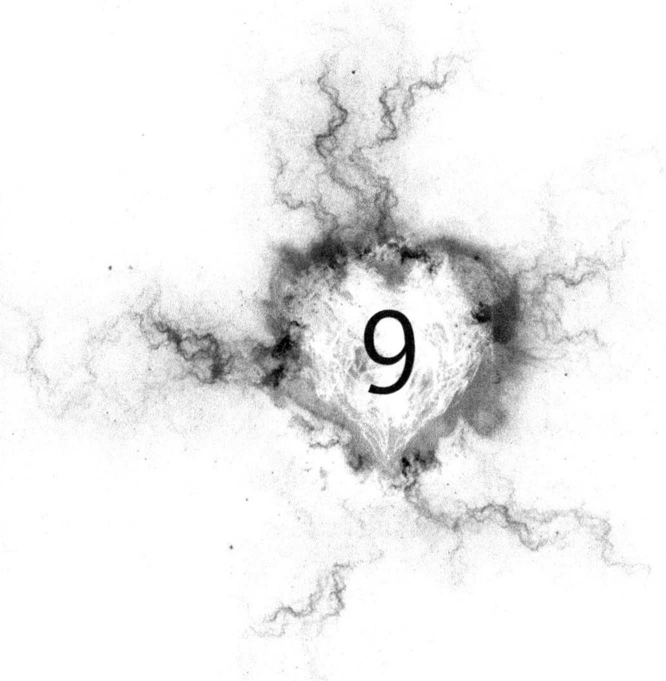

9

Awkward wasn't even close to explaining the thick silence that surrounded us as we sat at the table, waiting for Dad to return. He had walked the Crossmans to the door and was probably letting it hit them on the way out.

I had no idea how I felt, other than bombarded. We'd all been hit with so much information in so little time. I hadn't even mentioned that the Crossmans had also put me in a room with the guy who shot Dean, who was still in the coma I'd put him in, who they wanted me to revive.

The clinking of the teaspoon in Mom's cup reverberated through my skull. Rayni's powers had somehow managed to control my intake of emotion while Dean wasn't around, but it was different to the effect his presence had, and it had exhausted me. Or maybe the exhaustion was the result of having that whole kidnapping thing happen.

"Well, that was an all-new and unnerving experience." My dad walked back into the room with a business card in his hand. "I'm just glad you're back, and you're okay. You are okay, right?"

I looked between him, Mom, and Dean, all watching me intently. I nodded, clutching my hands in my lap so no one could see them shaking. "I'm fine. It scared me at first, obviously, but I get why they did it."

Mom scoffed. "I don't. How hard was it to come to us and talk first?"

I shrugged. "If I was the one they were looking for, they couldn't take the risk of me knowing they knew about me, you know? I mean …" I rubbed my forehead, trying to soothe my swirling mind and make sense come out of my mouth. "They were just taking precautions until they knew it wasn't me who'd been hunting empaths. This other empath *leech* sounds pretty dangerous."

I remembered all of the bodies lying motionless in the hospital ward—some put there by me, some by the leech—and a chill ran from my neck to my fingertips. I reached out for Mom's hot tea and drank some without even asking. She didn't say a word.

The silence returned as everyone seemed to ponder what *pretty dangerous* really meant in our changed lives.

Mom let out a deep sigh. "I think we need a break." She stood up and clapped her hands. "Come on. We need to get the shop fixed up, and I think we could use a distraction from all things supernatural. A bit of mundane work might give us time to think. If you don't mind helping out, Dean."

"Of course. Whatever you need done."

Dad nodded in approval. "I like that attitude. Lollipop?"

I pouted. Work was the last thing I wanted, with shower and sleep being much higher on my list. But I couldn't let Dean show me up to my own parents. "Sure. Fine."

Mom's emotional color-space had been a sickly green–orange since I'd gotten home, but a fragile stream of yellow happiness shimmered within it now. She waved us off to get ready. "Change into something you don't mind seeing ruined. I want to be on the next bus."

The whole ride to Mom's shop, Dean remained silent. The few times I caught his gaze it was intense, as though I could see right into his soul, see the war between his emotions and his denial of them. No outward sign of those emotions escaped. No wisp of color was visible.

The bus was full, cramped with the grumpy, the irritable, the overworked and the underpaid, smelling of body odor and dirty socks. Dean reached over and laid his hand on mine, pushing his blocking power a little harder, knowing exactly what I needed. Just his touch made me feel better, calmer than before. I mouthed the words, *"Thank you."*

Half the shops along the street were still boarded up after the quake and the damage those kids had done, smashing everything the shaking earth hadn't. Duck Egg Blue's front window had been temporarily replaced with a sheet of plywood, but I could still vividly remember the sounds of shattering porcelain coming from inside the last time I'd been there.

I could still hear Jake's charismatic voice ringing in my ears. *You're like me, like* us.

Inside, the shop had been cleared out. I didn't know how much had been broken and had to be thrown away, and what had been salvaged. I'd missed that potentially heartbreaking stage of the clean-up. There had been some structural damage too, and a couple of tins of paint sat in front of a freshly patched-up wall, along with brushes and rollers.

"Pick your weapon," Mom said, as she cracked open the

tin of blue-green pastel paint.

Dean picked up an edging brush, and I took a roller, my hands too shaky still for anything requiring precision.

For a while, we all painted in silence. Dean seemed to know what he was doing, and his steady hand brushed perfect lines of paint along the edges, his face a picture of meditative calm. He wore one of his usual gray T-shirts, and as he tensed to apply the paint, the muscles on his arms distracted me from my work more than once. While I began as tired and overwrought, soon the repetitive crackle of the roller moving over the wall soothed me. It felt good to put the strength and anger filling my muscles towards something that created a satisfying result.

Mom and Dad worked together on the opposite wall.

I broke the silence, words spilling from my mouth about how being pulled into an unmarked van made me feel, how I still felt bad that I might have hospitalized some of the agents who'd grabbed me, and what Limbus had shared with me about their leech problem.

"They have the people the leech has drained there, on life support. Along with guys from the gang, the ones who—the ones I—" I kept rolling one spot on the wall over and over with a roller long since exhausted of paint. "They want me to try and revive them, because if I can do that, they might have a chance of making the leech revive the others if he or she can be caught."

Dean put his brush down in the roller tray and took a paint rag to wipe where his line had just gone crooked.

Mom came over to tip some more paint into the tray for us. "So they want to train you, teach you, so you can learn how to do that. And it sounds like if you can, it would benefit everyone, maybe save some lives. But that's assuming everything goes the way everyone wants it to—that you learn how to do it, that doing it doesn't hurt you in any way, that those boys can be appropriately dealt with once revived, and that learning to revive them doesn't make you a target for this leech person."

"Wow." I stopped rolling. Mom had already projected consequences into the future much further than I had. "I hadn't really thought about the risks, as usual."

Dad dropped his brush into a bucket of water and wiped his hands clean. "You're a positive thinker, Lollipop, and a helper. And we love that about you. We understand you want to help these people, but we also want you to understand that you don't have to."

I nodded. "I don't know what I want. I'm just a little over-whelmed with things."

"Of course you are. It's been a whirlwind ever since you left the house to help out at the shelter." Mom took the unmoving roller from my hand, then gave me a tight hug. "We're all trying to figure out what our new normal will be. Just take it one day at a time."

One day at a time. I barely make it one minute to the next these days. But it was nice I had time to think about this decision. That I had people to take advice from. I had already raced into one negative experience, between my own yearning impatience and the empathic manipulation Jake had used on me. The very fact I was here, doubting and planning my decision with my parents, softened me to the Crossmans and Limbus some more. From what I felt and guessed, they hadn't even tried to use any compulsion powers on me to affect my choice. I'd felt none of that same warm befuddlement in the Crossmans' presence as I had with Jake.

Mom let me go. We had all stopped painting. Dean's lips were pressed thin and he looked away from me. Dad looked at the two of us, then patted Mom on the back. "Let's go check the inventory in the back room, just you and me."

"Subtle," I mocked, but I was grateful as he led her away.

I sat on the spotted drop sheet and picked paint from my hands. Dean sat beside me.

"You're worried," I guessed. "About the whole Limbus thing."

Dean shrugged. "I don't think that you working with Limbus

would be necessarily a bad thing. But I do worry about you."

And I worried about what him worrying about me did to him. I wanted to show him that loving someone could be a beautiful and happy experience, and not just one filled with pain and the fear of loss. That was hard when I kept getting into dangerous situations. Usually, people said that knowledge was power, but for some reason, with so many decisions in front of me, I felt like knowledge left me vulnerable and scared. How did I know which decisions would keep us from danger? And would they also be the *right* decisions?

"I could learn *so much* from Limbus. I could fix my mistakes."

Dean nodded, his gray eyes shifting back and forth between the floor and me. "Yeah. And if it all works, maybe we could have a ... better relationship."

My eyes immediately darted to him. As confusing as our relationship could be, I knew my heart belonged to him. But I had to admit things between us could be better, and to hear him admit it too was a big deal. "You're right. If I can give these excess powers back, you won't have to be on-duty all the time."

"And maybe I won't have the kiss of death." Dean *blushed*. He actually blushed. What world even was this? I didn't know, because the mention of kissing had wiped my brain clean.

Dean leaned closer to me, reaching out and running his hand down my arm. "But the question is, what do you want? It's your life."

I desperately wanted the kissing to start again right now, please and thanks.

I gave myself a mental cold shower and closed my eyes, bringing the question into focus. *What do I want?*

It was my life, but it had all felt out of my control until now. Before everything happened, my head had been in the clouds, dreaming of being a superhero.

Now I could really think about my future, and I really wanted to learn how to use my powers to the fullest extent. I wanted to be around people like me, people who weren't going to judge me or think I was crazy or turn out to be criminals. I wanted to make a difference, to help people.

"I'm sitting here weighing it out in my mind, but to be honest, I already know what I want to do. The moment the Crossmans asked me to help, I told them I'd try, and I meant it. I want to go for it. I want to figure out just how far this rabbit hole goes."

Dean half-smiled, but I couldn't feel his happiness. "I thought so."

"Honestly, the hardest part is going to be working out how

to explain any of this to Nati." I chuckled.

"I suppose you can't really tell her you're joining a secret superhero organization."

I frowned. I wasn't quite sure I was ready to call them superheroes yet. Not after my mistake assuming that last time with Jake. So far, Limbus had only described their work as dealing with empaths and freelance spy stuff for the government. Even at my tender age, I knew enough to be jaded over what that work could entail. But it still seemed like a good opportunity to learn. "What about you? I don't think Limbus knows about you yet, but I'm sure they'd be interested to get you on their team too."

He shrugged. "I'm not really a team kind of guy."

"You could be."

Dean hesitated, swallowing something down before shaking his head. "What if we hedge our bets? If they turn out to be a society of super-villains I'll be our secret weapon."

"I love a good plan B." The excitement of the afternoon, the thrill of having made a decision, and the surprising development that Dean could *blush* had left me feisty. I leaned forward on my hands and knees, bringing my lips close to Deans. "But let's hope plan A is a success this time. So the kissing can happen again soon."

Dean blushed again, and even the threat of a seizure wouldn't have been enough to keep me from him if my parents hadn't come back into the room right then to announce the working bee was over and pizza on its way.

I groaned at their perfect timing, sure they'd probably been listening in. But pizza sounded amazing, and I felt good knowing what I wanted. "Dad, you still have that business card? I've made my decision."

10

The Crossmans were openly pleased with my choice, and wanted me to come in again the next day to talk some more and show me around. I was doing mental gymnastics trying to work out how to get there. The Limbus building was an hour's train ride away from Bellscroft, down in the city of Bellston Main. I couldn't ask Dean to chaperone me all the way there and wait around to take me home again, and I couldn't risk him going into the empath beehive in case his powers were recognized.

Thankfully, Mr. Crossman offered to send their driver, and I made a quick decision. "Sure, but could you also send Rayni, if she's available? Just a bit on edge still after last time and might need her to do that calming thing for me again."

"We can probably arrange that." Some muffled noises on the other end of the line could be heard. Something about *class time*, *child safety*, and *building trust*. "We'll send her, along with her brother, to pick you up."

Dean and I waited outside the school gates the next afternoon. I paced, my backpack full of textbooks swaying on my back, and Dean leaned on the fence and watched.

"I can go with you if you like," he offered.

"And lose our plan B? No, I think you're right about keeping you secret for a bit longer. And remember to hold back, if you can, when they get here too."

A black SUV pulling up in front of us halted my pacing. The back door opened, and Ash and Rayni climbed out.

I raised my eyebrows, looking up and down the street. "What? No super-creepy grab-and-nab this time?"

"Again, super sorry about that," Ash said, with his usual one-thousand-watt grin. My lips twitched, wanting to return that smile. Now I understood him better, I found I missed his cheeriness since he'd stopped coming to school. Since his mission cover was blown.

He couldn't be much older than me, could he? Where was

the line drawn between training empath kids and creating secret agents? And was it weird that I kind of liked the idea of both?

"You were just doing your job," I replied, eventually.

"I'm glad my job wasn't being in that van. Man, the stuff the ops guys have been saying about you! Kind of wish I'd seen the action."

I raised my eyebrows at him.

"But yeah, ahem, super sorry."

Rayni pushed Ash to the side and dipped into a small bow that made her rainbow hair bounce. "Hi Olivia. I will try to do better for you this time."

She sounded so mature, and again wore a prim cardigan, but in pink. Maybe they were both older than I'd thought. "No problem. And you can call me Livvy."

As though we'd just become best friends, her grin shone in a way that completely defeated Ash's. Maybe she wasn't older after all.

"Ready to go?" Ash thumb-pointed to the car and the waiting driver.

"Almost, just waiting—" I spotted my dad walking around the corner from the street with the bus stop, and I waved to him. "Here he is."

I turned back to Ash's confused expression. "What?" I

grinned, enjoying myself. "You didn't think I was coming alone, did you?"

The Limbus building was tall, gray, and boring. It was a military-like structure with straight lines and few windows. There was a sign by the wide foyer entrance that said *Limbus*, small enough that it wasn't visible until you pulled into the parking area.

Although I'd seen some of it the day before, the stress of the situation meant I hadn't really absorbed what I was seeing. The parking area was open and surrounded two sides of the building. On one other side of the building was the deep channel of a stormwater drain, and on the remaining side, a vacant block, leaving the building appearing isolated despite being near the middle of the city.

Dad had chatted amiably to Ash and Rayni on the drive in, and they had done a good job of talking up the training and Limbus in general. They were technically boarding with Limbus, while both of their empath parents were 'out in the field.' I could only imagine what it would have been like to have grown up knowing you were an empath, with parents who were as well. Dad joked about coming into his own powers late, and hoping he'd get laser vision.

Only Ash laughed.

"Actually, empaths can't get laser vision," Rayni piped up like a grade-A student.

When we walked into the shining glass and polished timber lobby area, the Crossmans were there to greet us.

Hands were shaken all around and they began their tour of the facilities. Ash took his leave but Rayni remained beside me, taking her duty seriously. She didn't so much turn off my powers like Dean did. Instead she seemed to be controlling the emotions around me, making sure there was nothing too extreme reaching me in the first place. She made everything calm just by being there. Could she control emotions in other ways too?

The Crossmans led us to the ward where the drained were cared for, but we didn't go in. Standing outside the doorway, Dr. Crossman cleared her throat. "There's something we need to be open about."

Dad and I simply nodded, as we'd done to most of the information they'd given us so far.

"Jake and Jamie are our sons," she said, her voice calm and matter-of-fact.

"W-what?" I stuttered. Jake and Jamie who I'd run off with,

never even knowing their *full names*, were the sons of the Crossmans? I wondered if I should be doing a runner, but I wouldn't get far without Rayni beside me, nor could I leave my dad. *I wonder if I can carry them both?*

"I wanted to tell you before you found out some other way. And I want you to feel assured that we don't blame you or seek retribution for what you did. If anything, we are at fault for their behavior." She began walking again, as though she expected us to follow. She didn't go into the ward but continued down the corridor. "We knew what they were doing, and that it was going to end badly one way or another. We had been trying to bring them in for a while, but they were just too good at avoiding authorities. Which is also our fault."

Dad and I side-eyed each other, then trotted to catch up.

Mr. Crossman took over the story. "We used to be con artists. A family business, using our empath powers for greed— it's how we raised the boys. Then we came across a blocker."

My spine straightened. They did know about blockers. I gulped, remembering Jake's attitude towards blockers and hoping again they hadn't pegged Dean as one.

Rayni explained, "Blockers are a rare form of empath, and they have the ability to negate a proesthian's abilities or turn them off permanently."

I silently sighed with relief. If she felt the need to give me the textbook definition, it was doubtful they knew about Dean.

"The blocker shut us both down, Lola and I, permanently. We got away, but our sons outright abandoned us after that. Without our powers, they considered us lesser. Worthless. That was a real wake-up call for us."

No wonder they seemed awkward when I suggested they used their powers in our previous meeting. They didn't have any.

After a short elevator ride, we arrived at the door of a large corner office. A black leather desk had files spread out over it, and abstract paintings dominated each windowless wall.

Dr. Crossman stopped in the doorway, which had a brass label with her name beside it. "We ended up turning ourselves in. Mr. Kairu, the blocker, was a good man, and took pity on us. He was the head of Limbus at the time and gave us honest jobs. Taught us more about empaths than we'd ever imagined. He's also one of the victims of the leech.

"The point of telling you all of this is to hopefully convey that we believe strongly in second chances, and our great hope that the drained can be revived." Dr. Crossman swept her arm to invite us into her office.

"Thank you for your honesty," Dad said.

"I'll do what I can to help bring your sons back," I added.

Because *no pressure, right?*

Before we stepped inside, Mr. Crossman made a sharp inhaling sound. "Ah, I left some of the information sheets and intake forms we need down at reception. Rayni, would you—"

I was already shaking my head when Mr. Crossman realized as well. "I'll go get them. Actually, Mr. Mirawi, if you would like to come with me, we can go over some of them on the way back up. I'm sure it's the kind of thing that would bore a teenager."

Dad gave me a checking glance, but I nodded, and the two men headed back to the elevator.

Dr. Crossman still stood with her arm out, and Rayni and I went inside. Rayni took a seat on a lounge away from the main desk, and I could see she was looking tired. Was it from this extended use of her powers? Dr. Crossman ushered me to the cluttered desk and we sat across from each other.

I couldn't help looking at the files. A sheet right in front of me had a photo of a red-headed girl who looked familiar, and yet entirely unfamiliar.

I turned my head to the side and furrowed my brow. "Who is that?"

"That's Emma," she said, nodding to the picture as though she didn't mind me looking. "Although she looked quite different when you met her."

My mouth dropped open. Now I'd been told, I recognized her, but it was definitely pre-cosmetic surgery. It looked like a school yearbook photo from around middle-grade, and the face I knew was there, just less magazine perfect. But the most obvious of the spot-the-difference between then and now was, well, the spot. She had a huge mole, or birthmark, or *something* right across half her chin. I could only imagine how badly she got picked on for that.

"She had a pretty rough childhood, and it didn't help that her dad was more interested in collecting replica weapons than he was in saving his daughter from bullying." Dr. Crossman began gathering up the files, then gave me a thoughtful look. "How close were you with her?"

She'd offered to share her clothes. She'd been so excited to have another girl on the team. She'd called me 'sis.' But what had all of that amounted to?

I shook my head. "Not very. She was nice, but kind of flakey. I'm sure she was probably trying to figure out some sort of revenge when she was peeking into Dean's room at the hospital."

Dr. Crossman shook her head, then smoothed back one of her pin-up rolls of brown hair with a hand. "No, I don't think so. Actually, we just tracked her down."

"Where?"

"Not close enough to worry about. She popped up again a town over, in San Corale. We found her when she raised several red flags with the company she's taken a job with—this Three Minute Miracles service that hires masseuses to corporate events, parties, conventions, and so on. Sounds like she's using her empathic gifts to get a whole lot of extra money out of her clients."

"Yeah, that sounds like her all right," I muttered. "Are you going to arrest her?"

Dr. Crossman tapped elegantly manicured fingernails across the closed file. "We were actually hoping we wouldn't have to. We'd like to bring her in peacefully, if possible. She's young and has been misguided by … con artists. We feel as though she deserves a second chance. I was wondering…" She looked at the doorway, then back to me, lowering her voice very slightly. "Would you be able to talk to her for us? Ask Emma to come in peacefully? Explain the threat of the leech out there, and how we can help her, teach her the right way to use her powers? We are really hoping all it will take is a face-to-face talk with Emma, especially since you were, at least briefly, her friend."

Biting the inside of my lip, I saw the photo of the younger Emma again in my mind. My stomach gurgled. "Where exactly would I find her?"

Dr. Crossman slid a piece of paper across the table to me. "The Three Minute Miracles will be at this comic convention tomorrow. There is a cosplay party starting at three in the ballroom. Emma will be working there."

I looked at the sheet, taking in a deep breath. Carefully, I folded the paper and stuck it in my pocket with a nod. Doctor Crossman smiled and returned the gesture.

She put the files away and we were chatting more casually about the mix of empaths to non-empaths working at Limbus when Dad and Mr. Crossman returned, but my stomach still churned at the idea of seeing Emma again. If I did see Emma again. If my parents allowed it. If I told my parents.

I felt like I'd been given my first secret mission and I hadn't even received my superhero costume yet. Because while in the Crossmans' minds Emma might just be a misled young woman, in my mind, she was a villain.

11

"I feel as though I'm giving my child permission to join a fight club." Dad looked more than a little uncomfortable as Ash and I stood across from each other on a sparring mat.

We were on the ground floor of the agency in a large training room, with exercise machines, gym mats, and even a running track. Motivational posters had been tacked up onto the walls. Dr. Crossman had brought us there after suggesting we should end our visit to Limbus with 'a bit of fun.'

"There will be no attacks against Olivia today. She won't be harmed, and we'll all get an idea of just where she is in terms of controlling her powers." Dr. Crossman pulled out a tablet and stylus, ready to take notes.

"I'm the volunteer punching bag." Ash grinned, tossing a few juggling balls in one hand. He'd changed from the jeans and jacket he wore when picking us up to sweatpants and a tight tank top. He had the kind of tiny waist only a growing teen boy could manage to achieve.

They had offered me some gym clothes too, but I was more comfortable staying in my own outfit. The yoga pants and tunic shirt I wore were comfortable enough for a bit of action. I clenched and unclenched my fists, embarrassed under the spotlight. "I haven't, you know, had any kind of martial arts training or anything. This isn't going to be some cool montage of me being a kung-fu prodigy. I've only ever been in maybe four fights"—Dad frowned. *Aw, man. I should not have revealed that number*—"and I just reacted on instinct and scraped through."

Ash grinned, juggling the balls behind his back. "Instinct can go a long way, especially with superpowers backing it up. But regular training will mean having muscle memory to back up your super-speed, and knowing how to punch properly to capitalize on your strength. Then maybe you can be as awesome as me."

I chuckled. "Fine. What do you want to see me do?"

"Speed test?" Dr. Crossman suggested.

I nodded, but with Rayni keeping things cool and calm, I couldn't sense enough fear to use. "Um, there's no green energy around."

Dr. Crossman's eyes widened. "You get visual emotional feedback? You see emotions as colors?"

"Yeah." Everyone was staring at me now. "I mean, only since, you know, I ended up with the extra powers."

"Oh, I see. That makes sense. Some gifted empaths have that ability naturally, but it's rare." Dr. Crossman took down some notes. "Rayni, can you bring a bit of fear up in the room? Not much. We don't want to overwhelm Olivia."

Rayni looked pale and yawned, but she also nodded. "Sure. To who? Livvy's dad? Do you mind if I send you some emotions?"

Dad blinked a few times. "You can do that?"

"I'm an emogen. I don't get any of the cool superpowers like the primals. I kind of send emotions out to people. Just remember what I'm sending isn't really real, so just feel it but don't act on it, okay? Especially if I make you angry." She grinned a super-cute kidsy grin, like she could never make anyone angry.

"I'll try," agreed Dad. "I do pride myself on my emotional awareness."

Rayni nodded, and I could see a faint stream of green flowing from her through to Dad.

"Okay, this isn't a great experience." Dad looked like he wanted to vomit or bolt.

I focused on him, on the new fear flowing through him, and brought that energy over into me. Not too overwhelming, just enough. Only a hint of wooziness.

"Ready," I said.

Ash nodded, and without warning, he tossed all three juggling balls across the hall at once. "Catch."

One, two, three. I caught them with my eyes first, deciding my path. Then I sped after them. The first and second weren't far apart and I caught them easily, one in each hand. The third I pushed as fast as I could, blurring across the distance in a blink, and managed to fumble the catch because my hands were already full. I knew I'd been faster in the past, but between balancing my powers and hitting complete emotional overwhelm, I thought I did okay.

"Decent access to speed powers." Dr. Crossman made notes as I came back to the middle of the room.

Dad looked impressed and terrified. "Amazing, Livvy. I'd cheer but I'm worried I'm going to wet myself."

Rayni stopped sending him fear.

Next they had me do a strength check with a simple weights machine, recording how much I could lift while Rayni sent

Dad anger. He paced, fuming and muttering about second-guessing working with *these people*. Afterwards, Dr. Crossman had Rayni send Dad a range of subtle emotions, and asked me to pick them based on their color and my empath senses.

"Good, good. How about some fun now? Let's see if you can land a hit on Ash. Ash will act in defense only, and Olivia, feel free to use your full powers. He can take it."

Between using Ash as bait the day before, and letting him be a punching bag now, I wondered just how highly she thought of his skills. I guessed I was about to find out.

Rayni amped things up with a range of emotions going out to both Dad and Dr. Crossman.

Ash bounced a little on the spot and gave me a *come on, then* gesture.

My first swing was sloppy, timid. He leaned slightly to the side, crossed his arms and shook his head, his straight white hair shimmering. I tried again, faster, but without my full strength behind it. I wasn't close to touching him.

"Aw, *Lollipop*," Ash teased, like I was a child, grinning all the while. *Where had he heard that?* Right. It had been his mission to observe me.

Oh, it was *on*. My arms moved swiftly, chasing his dodges with my swings. The problem was, he was just as fast, if not faster. I couldn't lay a finger on him, let alone a hit. He'd had potentially a lifetime of training, and what did I have? Instinct?

But that instinct had saved my life in the past.

I let it take over again.

Our movements were so fast they would have been barely visible to a normal eye. I kicked out and he jumped. I jabbed left and he spun right. But then it happened. I caught sight of his eyeline—he kept his gaze on my fists and shoulders. I was projecting my every move.

So I projected again. When he reacted to my fake-out I ducked down and grabbed him by the ankles, heaved him skyward and slammed him down on the mat with a primal roar of triumph.

Followed by a hasty apology. "Omigod, are you okay?"

He laughed and waved my apology off. "Mate, pretty glad right now that you don't know how to punch properly. Ouch." He got back on his feet, gave me the thumbs up and walked off the mat, amused and, it seemed, sore.

Rayni clapped loudly, glowing golden approval showing at my defeat of her big brother. "Yay! Livvy is amazing!"

She had stopped sending fueling emotions out, but had also stopped calming the space, and her cheerfulness smacked me. "Oof, sitting down now." I swooned and landed cross-legged on the mat.

"Sorry!" Rayni squeaked, and quickly got things under control again.

I gave her a limp, long-distance high-five and gulped in air, winded from the fight. Dad and Dr. Crossman seemed to be taking a moment to recover too.

Rayni looked at me with glittery eyes. "That was so cool. I wish I was a primal too. Being an emogen is lame." She whispered the last word like it was a curse.

I scoffed dramatically. "Uh, no way. What you can do is amazing. You can control emotions! Of more than one person at a time. Like, wow. And you are so young; you have no idea where you could take it."

Rayni tilted her head. "What do you mean?"

"Girl, you reached inside me the other day strong enough to make my body think it was cool with just shutting down and sleeping forever. Which is terrifying, might I add, but also one super powerful superpower. If you can do that, imagine what else you could do."

Rayni looked thoughtful. "Still, your strength is awesome. Like you could lift a house and toss it on somebody."

"That would be epic," I replied, rubbing my chin. "Definitely putting that on my list of goals."

Dad walked over and put his arm gently over my shoulder.

"You're giving my daughter bad ideas. Next thing you know, she'll be on the news because she started throwing houses at people. Try to explain that one to the police."

Dr. Crossman muttered distractedly while looking at her screen. "Try explaining anything about empaths to the mundane authorities. They either think we are completely insane and try to lock us up in a mental ward, or they laugh us away. Hence the secrecy." She waved a finger in the air as though to demonstrate the entirety of Limbus around us. After a few more taps, she looked up from her screen and smiled, but it showed little pleasure. "You're quite strong, Olivia, with the additional powers in you, but also, it seems, highly reliant on calm surroundings or an emogen to support your unstable state."

"Yeah. Without help to keep this stuff under control, I'm basically a drooling mess." I winced, worried I'd said too much and given Dean away, but Dr. Crossman seemed to be focusing on her own tangent.

"I'm positive we can help you harness your abilities and keep them under control, until you can return your excess powers." Her eyelashes fluttered as she tactfully skipped over that those excess powers came from her sons. "From the drained we know of, Mr. Kairu was the third victim of the leech; his other victims all proesthians. Based on seeing your symptoms, I think the leech must have sought out a blocker to drain as a way to self-medicate, as it were." She seemed to be thinking out loud, but the implications sprouted scary thoughts in my head too. That there could be someone with all the strength of at least four proesthians like I had, but the inbuilt stability of a blocker as well. And that was the person out hunting for more empaths?

"I think I want to go home now," I said.

"I'm with you." Dad offered me a hand up. "That was one wild rollercoaster."

Ash and Rayni came with us again on the trip back, but we didn't talk much. From finding out the Crossmans' relationship to Jake and Jamie, being asked to talk to Emma again, and the thrill of test-driving my powers with other empaths—my head was spinning.

I could never imagine being so cruel to my own parents as to disown them. I loved my mom and dad, and superpowered or not, they were amazing. It was just another sign of the kind of people Jake and Jamie were. And Emma too.

The same Emma I'd been asked to find and attempt to deliver back to the agency.

I wasn't so sure about second chances. She deserved to pay the consequences for what she had done.

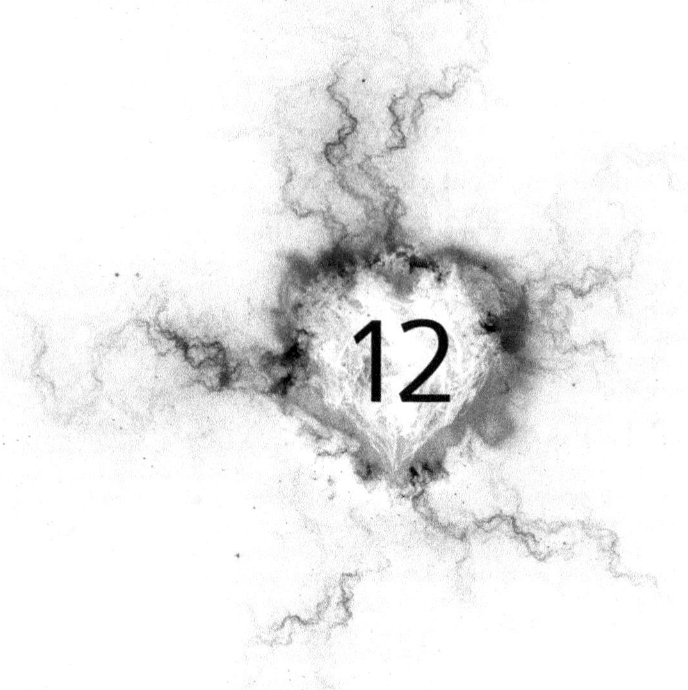

12

Dean met Dad and me on the garden path before we reached the front door. He had his hands deep in his pockets and his shoulders high around his neck. "How was it?"

Relief filled me at being back in his presence. Rayni did a good job, but she had been getting really tired by the end and the final part of the car ride had been rough. I wanted to hug Dean and soak all of him into me. "It was good. Exhausting. Lots to share."

I waved back at the black SUV as Ash and Rayni were driven away, then we all went into the house.

Mom had the same question for Dad and I as Dean did,

and I replied the same way.

"Sounds like your normal reply for every time I ask how your day was. *Good.* Not like you were just getting a tour of a clandestine society for superhumans or anything." She crossed her arms and pouted.

Dad chuckled. "Your mom's just jealous I got to go with you and she didn't. I'll tell you all about it, hon."

The two of them headed off into the kitchen with Dad giving Mom a full recap, leaving Dean and I alone. We sat in the living room, and I pulled a fluffy mohair throw blanket over myself, needing the comfort. I put the TV on a random cartoon channel for some cover sound, then gave Dean my own recap.

"They want you to go and see Emma?" Dean's pitch was a few tones too high.

"Shh! They asked me while Dad was out of the room. My parents don't know about that bit at all."

"And that's not a red flag to you? Don't you think you should tell them?"

"I won't have to, because I'm not going to do it anyway." I shook my head, the silky fibers of the blanket tickling my chin. "I've been thinking it through, and why should Emma get a chance join the Limbus team too, like we're all best buds? She had plenty of chances to do the right thing—at the bank, at the park, and probably a million times before that. She's a selfish fake and doesn't care about anyone, so I figure she can just keep on fending for herself."

Dean nodded slowly. "Could also be dangerous, seeing her again. Sounds like the best idea to not. But what are you going to tell Limbus?"

"I'm going to lie to them," I stated matter-of-factly. "I'm going to tell them that I *did* talk to Emma but that she refused to come in. That way, my job is done and I don't have to worry about Emma. Two wins, as far as I see it."

Dean tilted his head. "Couldn't you just tell them you don't want to do it? It's not like you're mission-ready yet or under their command. I'm sure they'd understand."

"But that could just end up with them sending someone else to go get her. Emma could still be part of my team again, which would be great to avoid."

"I guess. Look, you knew her and I didn't. And you've talked to the Crossmans more than I have too. If you think lying is the right—"

"I do," I said, too quickly and firmly.

Dean didn't say anything else. I searched him for any sign of emotion, approval or concern, but all I sensed was his usual blank chill.

I'm not wrong. I couldn't make the same mistake in trusting her that I had before. Just how many chances did someone deserve, after all?

My tour of Limbus had been on Friday afternoon, and the comic convention was that weekend. On Saturday, I fidgeted around the house, trying to let the day go by until enough time had passed during which I could have had a reasonable conversation with Emma. Mom and Dad were both out working in the shop, so when it got to half past three, I sat down with Dean in the kitchen and dialed Dr. Crossman's number.

"Livvy, it's good to hear from you. How are you doing? Did you get a chance to go and talk to Emma?"

"I'm fine, but ..." I wasn't even nervous. I'd rehearsed the script in my head so many times already. "I went and found Emma, talked to her, but she's not interested at all in joining Limbus. She's refused to come in."

Dr. Crossman let out a long, deep sigh. "You really tried your best to convince her? You have to understand, it's vitally important she come in. We can't have an empath like her, with a criminal past, continuing to use her abilities in those ways. We don't have access to a blocker anymore so we can't even shut her down for everyone's safety. You're sure you tried everything?"

"Yeah." I gulped.

"Very well. Thank you for trying." Some muffled noises at the other end of the line could be heard. Something about dispatch, refusal, and *neutralize.*

"WHAT?" I choked.

"I said, thank you for trying." I could hear the shuffling of papers and more murmurs of discussion. "Head home, Olivia. We'll sort something else out."

My heart dropped into the pit of my stomach. "Did you say...?"

Neutralize? But Limbus didn't have a blocker, so it wasn't that kind of neutralize. Maybe they were going to capture her and imprison her in some high-tech empath prison. My gut told me it was more than that, or that it could easily escalate to more than that if Emma made capture difficult. Either way, I didn't want Emma to die. I just didn't want her on my team.

Panic spread through me. Dean gripped my hand, questions wrinkling his eyebrows. What had I done? I didn't want to tell Dr. Crossman that I had lied. I had no idea what the punishment would be for that. Not to mention the fact that I wanted Limbus to trust me. I needed them so that I could learn to better control my abilities.

I had thoroughly screwed myself and Emma as well. There was no way I could admit my lie. But could I let Emma suffer because of it?

"Look, I can have another go. Maybe I can get her to come around."

"You aren't to approach Emma again." Dr. Crossman's voice was firm and chilling. "Things have changed. You should get back home as quickly as you can."

Cold sweat broke out on my forehead. "What's changed?"

There was a long pause of only quiet static on the line. "Olivia." Dr. Crossman spoke softly. "Ash is missing."

I gasped, and Dean held my hand, confusion all over his face. I shook my head and put the phone on speaker. "Ash is missing? Since yesterday?"

"After dropping you off, he had a date. Some girl I think you knew—Roxy? After the date, he never made it home. We've got agents out looking for him, but we are worried it was the leech."

"Emma's not the leech though. She couldn't be involved." My chest ached for Ash, and for Rayni. I couldn't understand how this had happened.

"No, but she's an empath flaunting her powers and could become an easy target for the leech if she isn't dealt with. We cannot, *cannot* allow the leech to grow stronger, which they do with every empath they drain."

Dealt with echoed in my ears. Dean's eyes were wide and his eyebrows low as he gathered what he could.

"We are working on things right now and when I have more news for you, I'll let you know. It is important that you follow the agency's wishes. Get home. Don't approach Emma again. Do you understand?"

"Yes."

"We'll be in touch." She hung up, but I sat there staring at the phone for several moments. I didn't know what to do or where to turn.

Ash was missing. Emma was going to be neutralized. I knew a secret empath agency would be serious stuff, but this was all too serious and all too soon.

One question wormed itself into my head, leaving my skin chilled. *What would Limbus have done if I didn't agree to join?*

13

"**A**re you certain she said neutralize?" Dean asked.

"One hundred percent," I said, throwing him a helmet and grabbing my own.

"And we're going ...?"

"Now. To Emma." I'd dragged Dean down to the garage but his understanding of the situation was lagging behind our bodies. Even my own body seemed to be acting before my head knew where it was at. After the phone call, I found myself throwing on my red trench coat and grabbing the convention address. It was only after we were at Dean's motorbike that I'd realized my decision.

I was responsible for leeching Jake, Jamie, and Donny. I wasn't going to be responsible for Emma being *neutralized* too.

My fingers smoothed across the shiny red helmet and I saw my reflection glaring back at me. "This is my fault. We have to warn her. There's no other option. They are going to treat her like a criminal and she's just a girl; she just made the wrong choices."

She did deserve another chance. I just didn't want to be the one giving it to her, but now I had to.

"Yeah. She can't be all bad. I don't know her, but I do know if she wanted us dead, she could have come into the hospital room that night and killed us right there. We wouldn't even have woken up long enough to fight back. But she didn't." Dean reached over and held my hand for a second, then put his helmet on and swung a leg over his bike.

I cringed as I put my helmet on. *What have I done?*

"Let's go. Fast. We've got to get to Emma first." I hopped on behind Dean and he revved the engine. "Just don't kill us, okay? Or I won't be able to beg my parents' forgiveness for this."

Everything in the neighborhood was quiet as the garage door opened. After a reassuring squeeze of my knee, Dean sped out. It felt like we were airborne for a second when we went from driveway to road. The back tire squealed as he turned, lined us up with the street, and we were off.

Dean gunned it, pushing the bike, and the road rules, to their limits. I wrapped my arms around his waist and we both bent forward, leaning into the ride.

The wind rushed all around us. Dean's focus on my empathic overload waned as he put all his attention to driving. On the bike, though, it wasn't that big of a deal. I caught wisps and whispers of emotion as we passed people on the street, but we moved too fast for anything to soak in. Which was a good thing, considering that a face full of asphalt awaited me if I were to fall and start convulsing. I closed my eyes and squeezed Dean tightly, feeling the hard muscles on his stomach tense each time we took a corner.

We made it to San Corale in only half an hour, a third of the time public transport would have taken. I pulled out my phone and loaded up the map to the convention center. Dean kept the speed up, bobbing and weaving through the traffic. I rolled with him, leaning when he leaned, becoming an extension of his body.

"There!" I yelled, pointing to a huge banner printed with *San Corale Comic Con.*

Dean pulled the bike up on the sidewalk as close as we could get, and we rushed inside. We pushed through the crowds of posing superheroes and families at the front entrance.

"Hey, Hey! You need a ticket," a woman in a high-vis pink shirt yelled at us.

"It's an emergency," I yelled back, and we ducked past the ticket check-point and into the main hall, scooting out of sight of security.

The number of visitors inside was immense. It was bursting with over-hyped children and irate parents and nervous fans. I reached back and grabbed Dean's hand. I couldn't risk being separated from him in here. Even with a direct connection to him my powers were *thumping*.

Dean held my hand tight as I practically dragged him along. I snatched a map out of the hands of someone dressed as a golden robot. "Sorry! Need this! Thank you!" I yelled over my shoulder, then scanned the map, trying to find the ballroom area.

I barged my way across half the main floor and off to the right where the entrance to the cosplay party room had another volunteer yelling at us for not showing a ticket.

"Where is she?" Dean asked, looking all around.

Everyone in the room was dressed up as someone or something from their favorite show or comic. Princesses and heroes, robots and soldiers, but now and then, between the colorful characters, I spotted people in bright blue shirts that had a logo printed on the front saying *Three Minute Miracles*.

I narrowed my eyes and scanned each one of them. They moved through the crowds, chatting in an overly friendly way to the other guests, or giving head and shoulder massages to them.

Up the back was a tall, busty blonde, her shirt incredibly tight, a diamanté covered fanny-pack slung over incredibly short shorts. She rubbed the back of a barely dressed barbarian and whispered in his ear. He looked entirely under her spell.

Emma.

It was the same wig she'd worn at the bank job.

We hurried in her direction. What was her reaction going to be? If I'd had more time, I could have eased into my reappearance in her life, but I had visions of a SWAT team appearing and whisking her away any second.

Emma laughed at something. Her eyes came up and met mine. Her smile dropped away.

Don't make a scene. We just want to talk, I prayed silently as we tried to get close enough to do so.

Emma backed up from her client, and her eyes darted around the room. "Stay back!" she yelled at the top of her lungs. "You monsters! I won't let you do to me what you did to my team!"

Every eye in the room turned to her, and then to Dean and

me. So much for not making a scene. It became quiet as the entire party watched, trying to work out what was going on.

"We're not the bad guys. We're just here to talk." I lifted my hands in peace.

"Talk to my fist, bitch!" Emma lunged, leaping from her position superhumanly high to land right in front of me.

Someone in the crowd yelled, "Aw, naw, she didn't!" and that seemed to be enough to make everyone think this was some kind of floor show.

When Emma jabbed her fist at my face and I dodged it fast enough to seem choreographed, the crowd broke into applause.

"Emma!" I shifted left to avoid an uppercut. "Really!" I blocked a head-height kick with my forearm. "Listen to me!" I thrusted both hands against her chest, shoving her back across the space the crowd had cleared around us. "You're in danger."

She skidded to a stop. The spectators cheered. I guessed it was better than them assuming we were in a real superpowered fight, but we had to get clear of here before someone got hurt for real.

Dean pushed through the mob and moved closer. I felt a chill extend from him. Emma's fists lowered and her face contorted. "No!" she bellowed.

She slouched like all strength had been sapped from her.

With a half sob, half growl, she plunged a hand into her shimmery bag and pulled out a small, silver gun.

My heart stopped.

No. No not again.

Emma pointed the same gun she'd wielded at the bank job, alternating its aim between Dean and me.

I stepped in front of Dean and wrapped my arms around him so he couldn't move. I couldn't lose him. I couldn't see him shot again. I'd do anything to stop that from happening.

Emma roared in frustration, and then threw the gun at us.

It plinked as it hit my shoulder then landed on the floor at my feet.

I exhaled and blinked. *What in all of insanity just happened?*

I slowly let go of Dean, somehow sure one of us was bleeding. We looked into each other's eyes, both uninjured and totally baffled. The crowd muttered amongst themselves, also confused about where our little performance was going with that development.

I stared at the gun for a long moment then picked it up.

It's a fake?

My head snapped up, seeking Emma. She'd pushed through the audience and was forcing open a locked exit at the rear.

I grabbed Dean's hand again and raced after her.

The door exited out into a loading dock, surrounded by stacks of cardboard and wooden pallets. Emma jogged past a parked forklift, but the area was surrounded in high fences and all the gates were closed.

"Wait! Please!"

Emma skidded to a stop, boxed in by crates. She looked like a cornered animal, her eyes wild and her blonde wig askew. "Just leave me alone!"

I stopped where I was, giving her space. "I don't know if you know about Limbus?"

Emma showed no sign of recognition, only suspicion.

"It's a secret organization of empaths, and they are coming for you. We came to warn you."

"Why? I don't know what you're talking about." Without taking her eyes off me, Emma leaned back and grabbed one of the gates, giving it a tug and a shake. Chained shut.

The alley extended down around a corner and out of sight, and Emma eyed that potential exit.

I called out, "They know everything about you. Everything you've done."

Emma froze. Her voice was a child-like whisper. "Everything?"

"But if we go to them before they come after you, I think you've got a chance."

"Oh, I don't know," came the muffled voice of an older woman. "I'd say you've missed your chance."

The voice had come from above us, and the three of us looked up the straight-walled convention building. Lined up along the roof stood a dozen figures covered head-to-toe in black.

Each had a large assault rifle, aimed at Emma.

14

I bolted with all my enhanced speed to stand in front of Emma. "No! She wants to come in. She never refused."

The figure in the middle of the team lowered her gun and bent her head to talk through some device on her wrist that glowed. "Olivia Mirawi and Dean Lasslow are here. Yes. Interfering with the target."

Emma whimpered. I kept my arms outstretched as though I could create a shield with them. "Is that the Crossmans? Tell them I messed up, that I never came to see Emma until now. It was a lie."

There was some more conversation I couldn't hear, then

each of the agents lowered their weapons, and stepped off the edge of the building. I gasped, but they all landed with perfect precision and continued to stroll toward us as though that first step hadn't been such a big one. "You kids are in some trouble."

Dean stepped over beside me, and the agents' march slowed. Some visibly shivered, and others stopped in their tracks.

"Are you sure?" I hissed to Dean.

"It's okay. They should know," he whispered back.

Unlike the younger empaths who might have never been in the presence of a blocker before, these older agents seemed to know exactly what was happening, and all looked at Dean.

"Is he—" the lead woman asked.

"Yeah, a blocker," Dean replied. "Which means you don't have to worry about Emma. If you think it needs to be done, I can block her permanently, instead of whatever else you had planned. She wouldn't be a threat to anyone."

"No," Emma cried out, dropping to her knees. "Please don't take my powers away. They're all I have. I can't go back to what I was before. Please. I'll do anything, join whatever secret club, do whatever I have to do. Just don't take my powers."

"Jesus," the lead woman spat. "Chill out, kid. Plans have changed. Boss is on the way."

"Stay put and get comfortable." A man told us. It was hard

to see who was who, because the uniforms they wore included silky balaclavas that covered their faces. Up close, their outfits seemed much more slimline and high-tech than normal police gear. They didn't have bulky flak vests, but still had large belts with many things holstered in various compartments. Near their wrists were soap-bar sized screens, with a slight curve to fit their forearms. Some had maps and info loaded on theirs. On others, the screens were black, with just a few small heart-shaped lights showing. They all looked ready for anything.

The agents spread out, some taking positions at the entries to the alley to make sure our business stayed private, I figured. A few more remained standing guard around the three of us.

Emma had started crying at some point and hadn't stopped. I sat on the oil-spotted concrete beside her and put my hand awkwardly on her shoulder. We still didn't know exactly what her fate would be. Or what ours would be. But I tried to be positive.

Dean sat on my other side, still breathing heavily from me dragging him around at superspeed. I probably should have carried him. I giggled at the mental image of me running through the convention center, cradling Dean in my arms.

Dean bumped his shoulder softly into mine. "You did good."

"You too. Letting them know what you are was really brave. I didn't want to put you in this situation. I wanted you to be free from the expectations of all of *this*." I gestured to the ninja-like secret agents surrounding us. "Aside from being our plan B. I'm sorry. You're here because I didn't do the right thing."

Dean smiled, shaking his head. "I'm here because you saw your mistake and did everything you could to fix it. If you didn't, if you didn't care the way you do, I wouldn't be by your side." He paused, licked his lips, and looked at his feet. "I love that you care so deeply."

Love? My heart made a whirring, thudding noise loud enough to echo off the buildings around us.

Actually it was a helicopter landing on a building across the street.

Felt like my heart though.

I held Dean's hand and we waited.

An agent opened one of the gates to the street with some kind of lockpicking gun. A couple more agents, in suits rather than tactical gear, walked in, followed by Dr. and Mr. Crossman. They marched toward us, looking really, really *cross*.

Dr. Crossman pointed to Dean and I and snapped her fingers. "You two, with us, now."

Emma looked up, her face streaked with make-up blackened tears.

"What about Emma?" I asked.

"She'll be going with them," Mr. Crossman said, indicating the agents waiting around us.

Emma tensed, begging me with her eyes, and I tightened my hand on her shoulder. I shook my head.

Dr. Crossman pinched the bridge of her nose. "She will be fine, I promise. I don't know what kind of impression you have of our organization that has led to this mess, but the agents here were only ever intended to bring her into protective custody, and would have done a much cleaner job of it than the drama you presented the convention with earlier."

"But you said neutralize. I heard you."

Dr. Crossman squinted as though confused before seeming to remember. "Well, congratulations on your excellent hearing, but you took that completely out of context. Now let's get you home before your parents find out and blame all of this on us."

I let go of Emma and stood up. She sat up and hugged herself. I felt bad leaving her there, but I tried to trust the Crossmans, and hoped they no longer had a reason to take things any further.

"This way," Mr. Crossman said.

Dean got up too and pointed the other way. "My bike is out the front."

"The agents will make sure it's returned to you."

We didn't argue anymore; it wasn't worth it. We followed them out and across the street to another building. It was a hotel, and I watched as one of the suited agents used their powers of suggestion to have hotel staff allow us all up to the helipad on the roof without an eyelid batted.

As we rode the elevator, Dr. Crossman said, "We seem to

have had something of a miscommunication. Or a number of them. But I thought I'd been clear on telling you not to get involved again. Like we don't have enough to worry about right now with Ash missing."

I hung my head, ashamed of the mess I'd caused. "I'm really sorry I lied. And that I thought you were going to kill Emma. They were really only ever going to bring her in?"

"Of course." Dr. Crossman sighed.

"And not hurt her? Even though you thought she'd refused to co-operate?"

"They would have used whatever force was necessary," Mr. Crossman admitted.

I nodded. I knew it could have gone worse for Emma if I had left things as they were. "She's going to be okay though now, right? With those agents?"

The elevator dinged and the doors opened to a windy rooftop. The sun was low across the city, glaring off shiny skyscrapers. A slim, matt-black helicopter sat still before us.

Dr. Crossman patted my shoulder in a stilted attempt to be comforting. "Now we know she was never against the idea of joining Limbus, Emma stands a better position than when we thought otherwise. Lying to us was a mistake, but you've proved you're a good person with how you reacted to what you thought was going to happen. Don't worry about the rest. The agents will clean everything up."

I flushed red with embarrassment. "I can't believe I thought you were going to have her assassinated."

The two suited agents headed over into the helicopter, taking the front. Mr. Crossman paused and looked back at me. "Your father mentioned you're in therapy, and I hope you continue to keep that up. It seems that your past traumas are affecting your judgement of current situations. You seem to be looking for the danger in everything."

The four of us headed over and got into the back passenger section of the helicopter. It was relatively comfortable, and I tried not to be scared as the blades started spinning. Maybe I really was looking for the danger in everything.

Dr. Crossman pulled her seatbelt on and spoke to Dean. "And as for you … I had a feeling you were more than just an overprotective boyfriend."

I glanced at Dean, mostly to see his reaction to being called my boyfriend. It didn't seem to faze him a bit. "Yeah. I only found out I was a blocker after Livvy found out she was an empath, so I really don't know much about this stuff either. Sorry we didn't tell you sooner."

"You didn't trust us yet. Understandable, I suppose." Dr.

Crossman's tone was soft and guarded. "Do you think you'd be interested in joining us at Limbus too?"

"Now you know about me …" Dean looked at me and shrugged. "Where she goes, I go."

"That's great to hear. A blocker is someone we've needed at Limbus ever since we lost Mr. Kairu, two years ago. Your skills will be very useful, and I'm sure we can help you develop them too."

Dean nodded, and the spinning of the blades grew louder.

I asked loudly, "What now?"

Dr. Crossman pulled on a headset. "Emma will be brought into Limbus headquarters. We have secure rooms where empaths of questionable safety can be kept."

I remembered the windowless room I had talked to Ash in, and the heavy-duty locking sounds the door there had made. Would that be Emma's life now? Imprisoned in that small gray space?

My own stuff-ups were leaving me feeling soft towards her, as much as the idea of her being at Limbus made me pouty. "We all have lapses in judgement sometimes."

"That's why we believe in second chances. What happens after that will be up to Emma now." Mr. Crossman put his headset on as well, and smirked. "And as far as your parents are concerned, we're happy to keep all this quiet if you are."

Lying had gotten me into this mess, but since it had all been a big misunderstanding anyway, and things seemed to have turned out fine, I figured this was one time my parents could be left out of the loop.

Soon the helicopter was too loud for talking. There were headsets for us too, but Dean left his off, and Mr. and Dr. Crossman seem to have switched to their own channel to talk to each other, so I took mine off again. I tried to enjoy the flight, and by the time we were nearly home a beautiful sunset had filled the sky with apricot and pink tones that reminded me of how Dean had blushed.

We landed on a sports oval two blocks from home and Dean and I walked back alone from there. After all the excitement, we were still home before six, and before my parents. We went in through the garage, surprised to find the bike already returned; the empath agent must have driven it back way faster than Dean had ever dared to go.

We had just started making some spaghetti for dinner when Mom and Dad got home.

"Do anything fun today?" Mom asked.

"Nah. Pretty boring, really."

My phone buzzed and I put down the wooden spoon I'd

been stirring the from-a-jar sauce with that was only for when it was my turn to cook. I frowned, seeing it was Dr. Crossman's number, and answered quickly.

"Olivia, I thought I should let you know, Ash has been found."

"That's great," I said. I met Dean's enquiring gaze and put my hand over the phone, relaying the news in a whisper to him. He nodded and quickly caught up my parents on the situation.

Dr. Crossman kept talking though, and all the blood drained from my face. "Oh no ..."

"What is it?" Mom asked.

"Ash, he's ... they have him back at Limbus, but he's been drained by the leech."

16

Dean and my parents chattered behind me, and I tried to focus on Dr. Crossman's voice. I hushed them, then put the phone on speaker.

"With your parents' permission, I would like for you and Dean to come in first thing tomorrow. We can send a driver. We need to take some precautions, keep you safe."

Mom's eyebrows twitched, then she nodded.

"That's okay," I said. "Could we visit Ash?"

There was a pause. "You can see him, but you know what state he'll be in. He's non-responsive. Although it doesn't look like there was much of a fight, his body was just … discarded.

Left out in the elements for almost twelve hours, so it might be a bit confronting to see him in that state."

Mom covered her mouth with a hand. She looked furious.

"We'll see you tomorrow." After sorting out the final details, I hung up.

I waited with stiff shoulders for my mom to explode, but instead, she just wrapped her arms around me and kissed me on the top of the head. "I know I'll have to get used to you being in situations less safe than a perfect plastic bubble, but this is all just too close to home. I'm too young to be this gray."

I hugged her back tightly. I remembered the feeling of pure grief and darkness I'd experienced when I drained the powers from Jake, Jamie, and Donny. It was horrible. It made my skin crawl. *But someone is out there doing that on purpose.* And had done it to Ash. Cheerful, grinning Ash. Maybe I had been paranoid about danger everywhere, but how could I not be with that evil out there?

The next morning, my parents waved us goodbye as the driver arrived out front. They had offered to come with us, but I'd told them we would be all right on our own, mostly in an effort to make them feel like things were fine because I was so obviously okay with everything.

When an unfamiliar driver got out, with no Ash and Rayni greeting us with smiles, I knew I wasn't really okay.

The driver was a stout man with an obvious combover and rosy cheeks. When he ushered us into the car, his face got even redder and he blotted it with a handkerchief from his back pocket. He wasn't very talkative, which was fine with me.

The entire way to Bellston Main, my thoughts swirled over the last few days. I wanted answers. Who could have done that to Ash? Would he be all right? Would we all be all right? As if Dean could sense my unease, he laid his hand across mine, calming the tension in my chest. We didn't talk, but we didn't need to. We both knew how each other was feeling, even if my empath powers weren't working on him.

The driver's nervousness rubbed off on me, and I checked the GPS on my phone a couple of times to make sure we were going the right way, but we always were.

When we arrived at the Limbus building, Mr. Crossman was waiting outside for us. The driver dropped us at the door and almost seemed to be relieved to have us out of his care.

I glanced at the retreating vehicle. "Is he all right?"

Mr. Crossman glanced at the SUV pulling off into the back parking lot. "Mr. Graybiel? He's fine. Kind of a nervous man, not a full-powered empath but very in tune with emotions. Maybe a bit too much to fit in with regular types. We thought a job here might help him feel more included and understood."

I chewed my lip.

"Not seeing danger everywhere again, Olivia?" Mr. Crossman tutted.

"No," I grumbled. But considering what had just happened to Ash, I was sort of surprised that the company head wasn't *more* alert.

Mr. Crossman led us up to the first floor and past the ward where the drained empaths were kept. Where Ash probably was now too. We entered a room a few more doors down, with a nameplate labelled 'Dr. Felix Slate, Esq'. Inside was a small lab, with multi-screen computers occupying a few desks that were also cluttered in wiry electronics, empty coffee cups, and a few overgrown house plants.

Dr. Crossman was already there, sitting on a desk and talking to a pale, gangly, goateed man in a lab coat.

"Morning," she said, looking like she hadn't slept a wink. Her normally perfectly retro-styled hair was loose and tangled down the back of her neck. "Glad you got here early. I need to go through this with you. I have a couple of other meetings to attend to shortly."

Dean and I stood shoulder to shoulder, both of us grasping our hands in front of us. Neither of us wanted to do anything wrong again so soon, and the gear in this room teetered like a tea shop a bull had already rampaged through.

The new guy collected some things off the desk and fiddled with them right up close to his face with one eye wide and the other squinted.

Dr. Crossman stood up and smoothed the wrinkles from her blouse—the same one she'd worn yesterday. "I'll get straight to the point. We want you both to agree to wear a special tracker and panic button device so we can better keep you safe."

That must have been the precautions she mentioned vaguely last night. Now I wished my parents had come in. Dad always had something to say about invasions of privacy in the digital age. It also felt something like a punishment. My nose wrinkled in disgust as I said, "You want to keep track of us all the time?"

"*For your own safety,*" Dr. Crossman emphasized. "It's been three months since the leech's previous victim, but that was in Bellscroft. And now Ash was found in Bellscroft as well."

"My town?" I'd imagined the leech as a shadowy figure prowling the alleys of the city at night, not strolling around my sleepy suburb.

Dr. Crossman nodded, her lips thin. "It could just be a

coincidence. We still don't know anything about who this leech is. But it's better to take precautions. We're not going to be listening in or following your every move, although we will station some agents permanently in Bellscroft. This will all be for 'just in case.' Just in case you need help. Just in case you go missing. We'd be able to locate you and be there to assist as quickly as possible with one squeeze of the panic button."

It sounded reasonable enough, but ... "I don't know."

Mr. Crossman sighed. "Trust us. We aren't the danger you keep seeing everywhere."

His wife rubbed her eyes. "Outside of your training sessions with us, we want the two of you to be able to continue your lives, keep going to high school, doing normal teenage things. The minors we have living in the building are only here because their parents are empaths as well, or they otherwise come from unstable family environments and are better off here. You two are better off at home, as long as we can keep you safe there."

I agreed with that at least.

"And we can only do that if you agree to wear the tracking devices." Dr. Crossman waved a hand at the lab guy, and what he was holding.

I checked in with Dean, and he shrugged. I had to make

the call. Maybe it was time I made the decision to trust these people. "Okay, I agree."

"Me too," Dean said straight after.

The lab-coat guy looked up at us then, but his eyes remained one wide, one squinted. "Hands please." His voice was way deeper than I'd expected based on his appearance.

"Sorry, I missed the introductions. This is Felix, one of our R&D guys," Dr. Crossman said.

Felix approached, holding a couple of rubbery wrist bands with a wide section at the front. They looked a lot like fitness trackers. He unclicked something to open them and dangled them before us. "Waterproof. Nearly indestructible interior fibers. Once I lock it on your wrist, it can't be removed by force by an attacker. I mean, unless someone takes your hand off. Let's hope that doesn't happen though! Press the front with your fingerprint until it turns orange to activate a caution beacon, or squeeze the two sides until it flashes red if you're in a real doozy of a dilemma. Also has a watch function. Pretty nifty really."

Dr. Crossman rubbed her eyes some more. "Felix will pair it to your fingerprints now. You can unlock and remove it with your fingerprint only, but we'd prefer you just leave them on all the time."

I took a deep breath and held my hands out. Felix took the red-colored band, pressed my right index finger to the top until it flashed green, then clicked it onto my left wrist. Dean got a black one.

"One tap turns the watch on and off. Three taps to unlock. Ooh, and you can even pair it with your phone to manage the watch features and some other cool stuff once you get approved for a Limbus account on the system." Felix's eyebrows bobbed up and down.

"Um. Cool. Thanks," I said, turning the watch on and off.

Mr. Crossman held up his own wrist then, showing off a gray tracker. "In case it makes you feel better." Dr. Crossman also pushed up her sleeve revealing a purple one.

Strangely it did, but also worse at the same time. Between the trackers, Ash, and Dr. Crossman's worried, sleepless appearance, the leech situation seemed more worrying than ever.

"Thank you for trying to keep us safe," I said, and I meant it that time.

Dr. Crossman nodded, and glanced again at her revealed watch. "I have to get to my next meeting. Walk with me?"

She didn't wait for a response, just started walking, and Mr. Crossman, Dean and I fell into line behind her. I waved a quick goodbye to Felix as we left him alone.

"Nice to meet you Olivia," Felix said, waving back. He looked intently at me with his one wide eye. "I'm really looking forward to doing some experiments on you."

"Umm, what?" I asked as we left the room.

Mr. Crossman half-smiled at my alarmed look. "He could have worded that better, but Felix enjoys taking on the air of a mad scientist. You will be working with him during your visits here to understand more about what's happening with your absorbed powers, and hopefully help find a way to give them back."

"Your case is very interesting to all of us, honestly. Yours and Dean's," Dr. Crossman added. "We have your brain scans from your hospital stay, but Felix has some more precise scanners, custom made for empaths. We're excited to find out what we can learn about helping you, the drained, and even stopping the leech. We are worried they have the potential to become very unstable now they've taken in more proesthian powers."

I looked guiltily toward Dean. "I'm amazed they can still function. I can barely stay conscious on my own."

Dr. Crossman left a small shimmer of blue in her wake, but didn't look back as she led the way. "We don't believe the leech has absorbed any more blockers since Mr. Kairu. Blockers ..." She glanced at Dean. "... are very hard to find, since their powers only manifest when in proximity to a proesthian. With Ash drained now, the leech must be pushing what their absorbed blocker abilities can handle. It could make him or her act more irrationally. Attack more often. But it could also be a weakness we could exploit."

A coldness stabbed at my heart. "But couldn't that mean that Dean's a major target to be drained? If the leech needs more blocking ability they could be hunting specifically for one."

Dr. Crossman stopped walking, and held up her wrist to display the tracker again. "Another reason we're taking precautions."

Dean didn't say anything, or seem worried, but I reached out and held his hand anyway.

"We're positive we'll find the leech soon though. Don't worry. Things have already made a lot more sense since your relationship to Dean's blocking abilities were revealed. It's helped our elucidists better read the situation."

"Elucidists? Is that another empath type I didn't know about?"

"You'll meet one at your first training session. I'm sure he can explain their powers to you then." Dr. Crossman glanced at her tracker watch again, but didn't start moving. An elevator dinged down the hall. She gave her husband a nervous glance, and then with a nod, addressed Dean. "There is one other thing that we hoped to talk to you about, Dean. We'd hoped we could address it later, but under the circumstances ..."

She trailed off. Dean raised his eyebrows. "Yes?"

"Knowing how you were able to block and then reverse the blocking on Olivia, we were hoping that you could possibly try to reverse the permanent block on us." Dr. Crossman frowned deeply, and her words came out forced, almost embarrassed. "I know it's a long shot but we could really use our powers now with the leech issue escalating."

Dean shrugged. "I'm not sure I could. So far, I really only understand my powers in relation to Livvy and ... my feelings for her."

Dr. Crossman, sighed and nodded.

"But ... I'll give it a try."

Dr. Crossman pressed her lips together and smiled. "Thank you," she whispered.

She checked her watch again, swore, apologized, then dashed off to her meeting while Mr. Crossman filled us in on what times our weekly training sessions would be.

We decided to catch the train home, not wanting to keep relying on Limbus's drivers—and maybe also to keep from being a bit weirded out by the last one. I was used to doing the pub' transport thing anyway. Mr. Crossman was fine with that, now we had our trackers set up, and even supplied us with company City-Trans cards for free tickets.

I trusted Limbus more now, but at the same time, fear continued to bubble in my gut. I could imagine those bubbles drifting together to spell out the words, 'Danger is Coming,' like some kind of prophecy

Or maybe it was just a sign I needed my next counseling session sooner rather than later.

17

The next week went by in slow motion. Dean and I went to school as normal. We weren't kidnapped, no roofs collapsed on us, and no new empaths were found drained. Once or twice, what I guessed was a Limbus van did a lap past school and my house, but it never hung around for long. Maybe they were keeping a protective eye on other empaths in the area too.

Nati was twitchy for a while after her brush with the kidnapping adventure, but soon returned to herself after I made up a story about mistaken identities and re-assured her that the person they'd thought I was had since been captured.

I wish they really had.

There were no new developments about the leech. I found myself itching to get back to Limbus for our first proper training visit. I wanted to stop feeling useless.

My parents ended up being pretty cool about the tracker concept. Dad even joked about wanting access to our location feed, but Mom told us they wouldn't invade our privacy like that, although thought the extra precaution from Limbus was probably a good idea.

When it came time to head back to Limbus, I could barely contain my excitement on the train ride. I hassled Dean the whole way there like a talkative squirrel.

"What do you think we'll learn? How many other kids do you reckon there'll be? How long do you think it will take me to work out how to put these powers back? Should we have brought some afternoon snacks? Is what I'm wearing okay? What do you think an elucidist is? We really can trust the Crossmans, can't we? Do you remember where the vending machine or cafeteria was from our tour?"

He shrugged a response for everything except for the question about my outfit to which he nodded, then blushed ever so slightly. I had changed after school into tight yoga pants and a red tank-top, and then, when I realized it was pretty cold out, borrowed one of Dean's hoodies.

Mr. Graybiel picked us up from the station, but the Crossman's didn't greet us on arrival at Limbus. A spectacled, frizzy-haired receptionist told us we were expected in the training room.

We walked through the doors of the gym, and straight away I noticed a guy just a bit older than us. He had light-brown hair and skin a very similar color, and his large ringlets formed a halo around his head. He was tall and heavyset, not so much muscular, but more as if he'd never managed to lose his baby fat.

Rayni was there too, wearing an oversized dressing gown. She sat on a mat at the end of the large room with two other boys and another girl, all at least as young as her. They all had downturned mouths, and blue auras surrounded them.

She looked up when we walked in. I waved, and she managed a small smile before it dropped again and she looked away. It physically hurt seeing her so sad.

The older boy walked up to us with his hand out. "Hey, I'm Sebastian. Olivia and Dean, yeah?"

"Livvy," I said, shaking his sweaty hand.

"We doing nicknames? Bastian, then," he replied. "Sweet to have some people my age around again after, you know, with Ash."

"Yeah," I said, noticing a blue aura around him too. "Is this it? All the students?"

"Yep, this is the class. Empaths aren't that common, really. Although I heard there might be another new student today too."

The doors opened again behind us as he spoke, hinges squeaking. My jaw dropped.

Mr. Crossman walked in, Emma right behind him. Another adult, wearing gym clothes, and a uniformed agent followed, the guard taking a post near the door.

My teeth clenched. I couldn't believe she was here already. She wasn't just some kid like the rest of us. She was a criminal. And they were just going to let her come and train with us? This was exactly what I didn't want.

From the look on Emma's face, she wasn't too thrilled with it either.

I tried to sound more curious than catty when I asked, "What is she doing here?"

"Emma has been very co-operative—"

I'm sure she's made it seem that way. I scowled.

"—so we think she's ready to join in. Bastian? We'd like you to work closely with her. We think your skillset and temperament would assist her greatly."

Bastian's eyes went up and down all of Emma, and he shivered awkwardly. He took a step backwards. "I can't work with *her*."

Emma's mouth made an *O* shape then slammed shut.

Bastian took a few large steps over beside Mr. Crossman and they both walked away, arguing rapidly and quietly.

"You two know each other?" I asked Emma.

"No." She sounded confused and fiddled with an orange tracker bracelet on her wrist. So she'd got one as well. She was protected too.

My lip twitched. "I can't believe they're just letting you off."

"Letting me off? Who do you think the prison guard is for?" she growled back, tilting her head to the agent at the door. Then she tugged at her tracker with her long fingernails, like she wanted to tear it apart. "And they have me locked down on house arrest with this thing. I'm far from free, which I blame entirely on you."

She glared at me, but I couldn't look her in the eye. I muttered, "Probably for the best."

Bastian and Mr. Crossman rejoined us, their conversation finished, and Bastian looking put out.

"Things don't always turn out how you expect. It will be fine. Train with her," Mr. Crossman said to him. He gestured for Emma to join us, and she hissed at Bastian as she passed him.

"Not like I want to train with an ug-fest like you either."

I wanted to slap her, but Bastian broke out into a charming, hearty laugh and squinty grin. "Okay, maybe I was wrong. I don't think we've got anything to worry about."

Emma seemed just as confused by his reaction as I was. Dean shrugged as well.

Mr. Crossman said, "Bastian is the elucidist I mentioned the other day."

"Oh, okay," I said, like I knew exactly what he meant.

"What the flip is an elucidist?" Emma snarled. Maybe it was good having her around, so I didn't always seem like the clueless one.

Mr. Crossman smiled. "Bastian, maybe you could show Emma a bit of what you can do?"

"Sure, boss-man Crossman." He unzipped his jacket and threw it to the side of the mat. His stomach pressed against his black tank top and although large, his arms had no visible muscles when he held them up.

"Emma, if you would like, please attack Bastian. Feel free to really go for it."

"Don't have to ask me twice." She flexed, and I could see colorful streams of emotions flowing into her from sources around the building, including fear from me about what Bastian was about to suffer.

She moved at blinding speed, red hair flying behind her,

not holding back a bit. Maybe she thought this was her chance to show off, like this was a prison yard and she had to punch the biggest guy in the room. I winced, but Bastian ducked and swayed effortlessly away from every blow, bending like one of those inflatable dancing men outside of car dealerships. While Ash had been always a step ahead of me in our match, Bastian was five steps ahead of Emma without even using any super-speed.

She soon slowed down, eyes wide, teeth bared, sweat glistening on her forehead. She grunted, landed on her bum and smacked the mat with her fist.

"That was incredible," I said, still in awe. "How did he do that?"

Mr. Crossman smirked. "Elucidists can read people's emotions, much as other empaths can, but to almost precognizant levels. Emotions affect every decision people make, and elucidists can get a sense of someone's actions and choices even into the future."

"Wow, that's some next-level stuff," said Dean, looking impressed.

I side-eyed Emma, frowning. Is that why Bastian reacted to Emma like that when he first saw her? Just what did he sense in her future that he thought was so bad, but Mr. Crossman thought wasn't an issue?

Emma flopped back onto the mat and face-palmed. "Future vision? For real? No fair! I must have looked so dumb!"

"Who cares how you looked?" Bastian shrugged.

Emma pouted her surgically enhanced lips, and she flushed red as her hair.

Mr. Crossman explained, "Elucidist powers are effective for short-term decisions, like which way an opponent is going to swing. But anything more down the track is often wrong. People's emotions and decisions can be changed or influenced by even the smallest things. But it can give us some ideas about what paths they might take." His tone was pointed.

Bastian begrudgingly offered Emma a hand and helped her off the ground. "Good match," he said, sounding like he meant it.

"That was pretty cool. I suppose. I'd never heard of elucidists before," Emma muttered.

Mr. Crossman excused himself and the gym instructor took over. He gathered all the students together, had us take a place on the mat, and follow him through a range of physical and meditational exercises. Some seemed very tai-chi-like, with a focus on centering our minds, developing a greater connection to our own bodies, and extending the reach of our senses in that calmed state. I awkwardly twitched through the elegant movements and fidgeted when we were meant to still our thoughts. Dean was a natural.

I kept my eye on Emma the whole time, but she seemed to be diligently following the instructor's directions, although she glanced sideways at Bastian a couple of times and glared at me a few more.

When training wrapped up, I grabbed Rayni before she left and gave her a huge hug. "I'm off to see Felix now for some tests. I'm sure we'll work out a way to restore the drained empaths. Then Limbus will find that leech and make them put your brother back."

Rayni sighed like she'd heard it a million times, and managed to twitch up the corner of her mouth. "We'll all do our best."

Bastian remained in the gym with Emma, sitting cross-legged as they faced each other on a mat, talking. I was comforted to see the adult agent still keeping an eye on her too, before Dean and I headed up a floor to the labs.

I felt good after the training, more focused and calm. Until I walked past the intensive care ward. The double doors had been left open, and inside I could see all the drained empaths in their beds. Two nurses moved around the room, rolling the corpse-like patients onto a different side to prevent bed sores. In the closest bed was Ash, his face as white as his hair. The cat I saw before was curled up asleep near his tucked-in feet. I swallowed hard. Seeing someone who had been so cheerful, so full of life and energy lying so still, felt like looking into a shattered mirror to some twisted, alternate dimension. I couldn't fathom it, what void they were trapped in. Could they sense anything? Or were they simply shells now?

I turned away, and Dean moved closer, his shoulder pressed to mine and our fingers entwined as we continued down the corridor.

We headed to the examination room, right next to the one where we'd met Felix last time.

The door was open and Felix waved us in, distracted by the circuit board of what looked like a CT-scan machine. There were three other high-tech medical machines in the room I didn't know the names or uses for, and a small side room behind a pane of glass filled with monitors.

"Hi Felix," I said nervously. He wasn't particularly old, but I felt odd calling him by his first name knowing he was a doctor.

He turned around to eye me for a second. "Oh, we are going to have some fun today."

He returned to the machine and I gave Dean a worried look, then hid it when Felix spun toward us. "You, there," he said, pointing to Dean and then an office chair in the sectioned off area. "You, there." He pointed from me to the bed of the CT machine.

Dean squeezed my hand then we went to our positions. I wriggled up onto the beige vinyl-padded platform. "Do I need to take off any jewelry or anything?"

"In case it gets ripped off you by the awe-inspiring power of magnetism?" Felix bellowed, then waved a hand dismissively. "No, not today. Different kind of thing."

I laughed nervously. "You've got an interesting bedside manner."

He stroked his goatee and looked at me with his uneven eyes. "Really? No one's ever mentioned it before."

He pumped some hand sanitizer from a dispenser on the wall then stood over me, placing small, round, sticky papers across my forehead. He clipped several wires onto each. He adjusted the last one and mumbled, "Don't worry. This will hurt me more than it will hurt you."

"What?"

"What?" He shrugged like he had no idea what I was talking about and backed away. He joined Dean in the sectioned off room, watching from behind the thick protective glass.

The hum of the machines startled me. Felix's voice came through a speaker next to my ear. "This will only take a second.

You won't feel a thing. Aaaaand okey-dokey off we go-key."

The donut-shaped section of the machine lit up bright blue and the platform I laid on adjusted and moved into it. I licked my lips and tried to stay still, but ended up talking nervously. "I imagined learning to control my powers would involve stuff like meditating under waterfalls. I didn't realize how high-tech it would be."

The speaker buzzed again, and this time it wasn't Felix, but a pre-recorded voice of a sweet-sounding woman, directing me when I should hold my breath and keep still and when I could move again. It ran a few cycles and then Felix opened the door and said, "Hey! Do you want to see your BRAIN? Come on. Just rip those things off."

I blinked and sat up, unclipping the wires and leaving them on the bed.

"How was it? Okay?" Dean asked, as I walked in and flopped down in the third chair. He reached over and helped me pick the sticky tabs off my forehead.

"Yeah, no problem."

Felix tapped at a keyboard, and the large screen in front of him had a pretty generic-looking medical image of what I guessed was part of my brain. I didn't know the terminology but I knew the gray squishy stuff was important.

Felix coughed into his fist and pointed at the screen. "Check this out. It's exactly what I was hoping to see." He hit a button, and the cross-section view of my brain lit up, sparkling like a nebulous galaxy. "Your limbic system is firing up with four unique bio-electric signatures."

I couldn't quite see what he was referring too. "You mean you can see me, Jake, Jamie, and Donny all in there?"

"Bingo! Which it proves my theory was correct and I'm a genius."

"What theory? That I now have three extra dormant personalities?"

Felix smiled cheerily. "Yes! But that's good. They are all still there, all intact, and all distinct. It's great news. A bit more work on focusing and developing your powers, and you should be able to separate all three boys from your mind and expel them back out again where they belong. Imagine it." He looked up at the ceiling for a moment as if doing exactly that, then smacked his knee and laughed. "Imagine you sent the wrong consciousness back into the wrong body! Classic!"

I gulped. Great, there was an all-new terrible outcome I hadn't worried about yet. If I even could shoot bio-signatures out of me. "My powers have been all more on the absorbing end than the, er, expelling end."

"Pretty typical for a proesthian."

"Is that what you are too? Or—"

"Just a regular old Joe here, if Joe were a *mad genius*. My mother was an elucidist but it didn't pass to me. Lots of folk in Limbus aren't empaths, but know about them for some reason or another. Nice to help out with the super side of things though. My mother always said, 'In times of trouble, look for the helpers; they are the ones most likely to have candy in their pockets.'" He plunged a hand into a pocket of his lab coat and pulled out a handful of cat kibble, then put it into a small silver bowl in the corner.

A second later, the black and white cat I'd seen before ran in, wound around our ankles, and started eating.

I reached over and ran my hand through its soft fur. It purred but didn't stop eating. "What about the cat? Is it an empath?"

Felix glanced back. "Kimmy? She used to be Mr. Kairu's cat. Still is, I suppose. I just keep the fluffball fed. She spends most of her time sleeping on the beds with the ICU patients. I think cats are natural empaths of a sort. They even have their own superpowers."

"Really?" I asked.

"Oh yeah. Their purr is at a sound frequency known to heal bone and muscle injuries. Pure scientific magic. You should hear Kimmy purring away in ICU. I'm sure she's trying to help them."

Kimmy mewed then hopped up onto my lap, kneading my thighs and purring loudly. I leaned down and touched my nose to the top of Kimmy's head. "Good kitty. They can use all the help they can get."

18

I broke down crying for almost all of my next therapy session.
We'd just started, still in small-talk mode, when I suddenly
wondered whether Jake, Jamie, and Donny could still experience
anything inside me. If they were able to observe my actions,
my time with Dean, or my parents, or what I said privately in
counseling. Then I was thinking about what I did to them,
and Ash, and the leech, and trackers, and Emma, and *danger,
danger, danger.* Then I was sobbing.

Debbie let me cry, and I'd only just pulled myself back
together when time was up. I switched with Dean for his
session and hoped my face wasn't too puffy and red as I sat

to wait outside.

There was a ton of foot traffic moving through the mental healthcare facility that day. I frowned as a couple of nurses ran past. *It's probably nothing. Stop looking for danger everywhere.*

Two doctors walked past the waiting area and stopped, oblivious to me sitting there.

"He's always been non-verbal," one of them said. "But I can't find any medical reason for his deteriorated condition since lunchtime. He is completely non-responsive. It's too early to say but it seems like a coma."

The other doctor grunted. "Has Holbrook's medication been changed recently?"

A memory flashed through my head of the old man who'd made me feel cold. On the front of his shirt he wore a tag that said Holbrook.

He was really old, I tried to reason with my gnawing paranoia, but my body was already alert, trying to hear more. I pretended to be entirely engrossed in the two-year-old health magazine I'd been flicking through and leaned closer.

"No change to medication," the second doctor replied. "Sad, really. Poor guy had such a hard life; his extreme chronic depression was understandable. And now this."

"Let's get some tests run. A person doesn't just slip into a coma for no reason."

"No, they don't," I whispered to myself.

I watched the doctors walk away, sat up straight in the plastic chair and put the magazine away. My mind was screaming. *Holbrook was a blocker. The leech got him.* I took a deep breath and tried to calm myself down. This wasn't necessarily empath stuff. There were a lot of other possible explanations. How could I tell this wasn't just my danger senses misfiring? But everything in my churning gut said something bad had happened, was happening here.

I clutched my hands together tightly on my lap and attempted to do nothing but calming meditative activities until the door beside me opened again and Dean stepped out.

Debbie said her goodbyes to Dean then smiled at me. "I hope you're feeling better, Livvy. Keep up your mindfulness exercises, and remember I have lots more resources available for you if you need them."

I cleared my throat and tried to use my calmest voice. "Actually, there was one thing I was thinking about that I'd like to try that I think could really help ground me."

She raised her brow. "Really? That's great."

Dean's forehead wrinkled as well but he didn't say anything.

I nodded enthusiastically. "We passed by the common area

on the way in, and it looked like a really nice environment, and I thought maybe Dean and I could spend a bit more time here. Maybe even chat with some of the other patients, get a bit of perspective."

I held my breath, hoping that the therapist didn't think it was strange, inappropriate, or weird. After a few moments, she grinned, then waved for us to follow her to a reception desk nearby. "Mary, can you get me two visitor passes for the general ward? Thanks."

She turned back to me. "You've shown great maturity in our sessions, Livvy, and I trust you will again in any interactions you have with our residents. But I agree, it could be a healthy exercise for you both."

I wasn't sure if she thought it really was a good idea or if she was just taking pity on me after my big sob-fest. Either way, I thanked her, and we took our visitor passes and made our quick escape.

When we were out of earshot, Dean said, "You want to spend more time here? Why? Did you see something?"

I explained what I'd overhead from the doctors.

Dean listened but didn't reply.

"Okay, I know, I know. Livvy and her crazy conspiracy theories. Just humor me? Again?"

Dean looked at me thoughtfully with his cold gray eyes for a long moment. "Sure. What could go—?"

"No! Shh! Don't say the famous last words." I made a mouth-zipping gesture.

Dean half smiled, and we reached the entry to the common area.

Large windows made up an entire wall of the long room, and filled the space with cheery sunlight. Brightly coloured bouquets of gerberas filled vases in the middle of large tables that had board games and craft supplies spread on them. I spotted several carers wearing brightly colored uniforms, some interacting directly with residents, joining in the activities, others roaming and keeping an eye on things. One checked our visitor tags as we walked in.

About ten patients sat in armchairs up one end of the room watching a romantic comedy on a big screen. The remaining few residents were spread out, mostly alone or in pairs. Some wore basic scrubs, but the majority wore comfortable-looking everyday clothing.

Dean stayed close behind me, shielding me from the barrage of emotions that the place brought. "What are we looking for?"

I tried my best to remember. *Someone petite and blonde, and from a distance, basically androgynous.* In the corner, I saw a boy-faced girl with the sides and back of her blonde hair buzz-cut, leaving only a tangled swirl on top.

"Her." I nodded in that direction.

The tiny, curve-less girl was maybe fifteen, wore scrubs, and sat perched on the arm of a floral-patterned recliner occupied by a middle-aged woman. The elder of the pair had short gray hair, dark-olive skin and a slouchy, rounded shape, mostly hidden under a knitted blanket. Her eyes were shut, her mouth closed but smiling, and as we approached I heard her humming a cheerful tune. Tiny wisps of yellow happiness spread from the woman toward the blonde.

"Hi," I said timidly. "Mind if we join you?"

The girl's eyes met mine, then Dean's. She full-body shivered and her face scrunched up. She looked like she wanted to run away. Then she tilted her head and stilled.

"You made everything stop," she said to Dean.

Dean's jaw dropped open.

"Told you," I mouthed when he looked my way.

The girl squinted at us both. "Pull up a chair. Docs say I need to be more open, but they don't know what it's like. People are much *much* too much. Normally. You two are different."

We're like you, I wanted to say. But I had to be careful. It made sense that without understanding their powers, and without support, empaths could easily become emotionally unstable, diagnosed as who knew what and locked away. It made me feel good to have Dean there with me. I knew if anything happened, he could shut their powers down.

We dragged over a couple of plastic chairs.

"My name's Livvy, and this is Dean."

She eyed our visitor tags. Her eyes were dark, matching the circles beneath them. "I'm Sway. This is Marigold, but she doesn't talk much."

Marigold opened her eyes then, woken by her name. She looked at Dean, and shivered violently, despite the warm sunlight streaming down on us all.

Dean and I shared another glance. She felt his blocking power too.

Marigold pulled the blanket up tighter around her as though it could ward off his effect and turned away from us to look out the window.

Sway put a hand on her shoulder. "She's not being rude. Goldilocks is all sunshine and lemon drops normally. If only you could *see* ... but I think they've fried her with all the drugs she's on." Sway's eyes roamed around the room. "All the colors have stopped too."

I leaned back in my chair. She saw colors from emotions

too? Did that mean she'd absorbed other empaths like I had? It couldn't be that she was the leech … Sure, she could have gotten Holbrook, but not the others. I wasn't sure she'd been out of this building any time recently. Dr. Crossman had said some rare, highly talented proesthians had the color vision naturally. I hoped that was the only reason she could see emotions in shades like I did.

"Colors?" I asked, innocently.

"Bless me. It's my kind of crazy. A cute, curly, swirly kind they haven't found a label for yet." She twitched and slapped her ear.

Empaths. That was the label they should have, one that could actually help them. And I was sure now the man in the coma was one of us as well. That also meant there was a good chance all of their lives were in danger.

Sway reached into her shirt, pulled out a plain cookie and started nibbling on it. When she saw me staring, she ducked her face away. "They don't allow food outside of mealtimes."

A carer walked over and Sway stuffed the cookie down between Marigold's blanket and the arm of the chair.

"Time for group, ladies," she said, clapping twice.

Marigold started moving immediately, getting to her pink-fluffy-slippered feet and shuffling away, taking the blanket with her.

Sway groaned and slumped into the spot Marigold had left.

"Don't care. Group's not fixing my crazy, crazy, crazy. Momma used to say I was too crazy for the Lord."

"Come on, Sar—"

"Sway!" she barked.

"*Sway*, we don't want another incident, do we?" The carer seemed to notice Dean and me then, glanced at our visitor tags, and gave us an apologetic look as though she was sorry we had to see this.

Sway held out an arm as though inviting the carer to drag her away, which she did, in a gentle way, sighing audibly.

"We have to do something for them," Dean said.

My pounding heart was relieved he was onboard. "We really do. Because what if the leech has discovered that this is a good place to pick off undiagnosed empaths?"

Holbrook's 'new condition' had begun only that morning. My heart reached out for Sway and Marigold and I wanted to race after them, tell them what they were, keep them safe.

I turned to Dean and murmured the fear that had swelled inside me. "And what if the leech is still here?"

19

Dean and I left the common area and went down a quiet corridor for some privacy. I leaned against the stairwell door. I tried calling Dr. Crossman but it went to voicemail. I tried again. Same result. I started pacing, biting my nails, then noticed my wristband. "I'm going to try this out."

"Are we in a panic button situation?" Dean asked, fidgeting with his own tracker.

"I'll use the caution beacon. Hopefully that's enough to get Limbus's attention. We need to get them down here fast." I pressed my fingertip to the top of the tracker and waited until it glowed orange.

Not two seconds later, my phone rang. Dr. Crossman's name was lit up on my screen. I put it on speaker. "Olivia, are you all right? Did you mean to set off your caution beacon?"

"We're okay, but we're worried there's an issue here."

Dr. Crossman hesitated, and I heard some typing sounds. "You're at the Bellscroft Mental Health facility? Your location came up as soon as your beacon activated. Did something go wrong at your therapy session? The tracker really is only to be used for dangerous situations."

I could hear the patronizing tone in her voice. "I know. I pressed it because I think there are empaths here, some of the residents. I mean, I know there are. This isn't me being paranoid. Please trust me."

"Okay, it's something we can look into. I have contacts I can check in with to see—"

"No, you've got to come right now. One of the patients that I thought was a blocker? He was found in a coma around lunchtime."

"Today?" Dr. Crossman asked urgently. I heard more typing. I stared at the phone I held face-up in my palm. It had only just ticked over to three.

She didn't wait for an answer or for me to explain my fears. She got it. "We'll send agents right away. Find a safe place to wait. A crowded waiting room or something. We've got agents ten minutes out and I don't want either of you on the street alone."

A strange, harsh smell made my nose wrinkle. *What is that?*

When I didn't answer, Dean agreed, bringing my attention back to the conversation.

"Who were the other patients you think could be empaths?" Dr. Crossman asked.

"A girl going by Sway, probably with the real name of Sarah, and a woman called Marigold." I ran over a quick physical description for both as well, and as I did, the smell grew. The smell of something burning. We began to head off to find a waiting room, however, as my feet shifted, movement caught my eye.

Tilting my head to the side, I walked forward, stopping a few steps away from the emergency stairwell doors. Rolling gray smoke floated across the floor.

Suddenly, the fire alarm began to blare. Lights flickered overhead.

Sickly green energy seemed to seep toward me from every direction. Fear, so much fear. Dean grabbed my hand.

Dr. Crossman's voice was urgent. "Livvy? What's going on?"

I opened my mouth to speak when the door to the stairwell blew out, slamming against the wall. Flames shot from the entrance. I was hit by a wall of hot air. I pulled Dean away from the licking flames and we ran down the hall.

"There's a fire!" I yelled into the phone. Sprinklers went off, pouring cold streams of water over us.

"Get out of there! Take no chance … to … the …"

I furrowed my brow and tapped my phone against my palm. The screen was soaked and went black. The smoke chased us down the hallway.

The sound of glass smashing and people yelling came from all around. We saw more flames up ahead. The fire burned so hot that the water from the sprinklers didn't even touch it.

We took the next turn in a different direction, skidding on the wet carpet. A thin gauze of smoke surrounded us. People ran past the intersection up ahead.

I stopped at an emergency sign stuck up on a wall, squinting at it through watering eyes. The markings were all blurry.

Dean tugged at my hand. "We have to get out of here, Liv. The whole place is going up."

I heard coughing, and looked into the room beside us. A man sat still in a wheelchair, with no real idea what was going on. I ran over and grabbed the chair, then sped back to Dean. Even with him there, there were enough emotions swirling within the smoke for me to absorb. For the first time, I could almost section out the influx, reading its source, floor by floor. My chest bulged with the feelings of fear, anger, and, there it was … relief. Taking in a smoky breath, I focused, sorting the emotions like color charts in my mind until I could see where the relief was coming from.

"This way," I yelled, my throat burning.

He nodded and I led the way, pushing the wheelchair in front of me. Around the next corner, a young woman was huddled, screaming against the wall. Dean took over pushing the man, and I threw the woman over my shoulder. We kept running. At the stairs, I used one hand to help Dean drag the wheelchair down. We ran out of the stairwell to the right, and through the exit door.

Patients and staff spilled in all directions over the concrete-covered outdoor area, relief all around at being out of the building. Fear and sadness mingled at how the structure roared and crackled, the flames engulfing it.

I put the woman down, still screaming, next to a nurse who was checking on some other people, and Dean parked the man in the wheelchair beside her.

I searched for Sway and Marigold.

I couldn't find them.

I spotted the nurse who'd taken them away for group.

"Where are Sway and Marigold?"

Her head snapped over to a small crowd of patients behind her and then up to the second floor. My eyes followed.

She stumbled over her words. "They—they should be here. In the panic, maybe they got separated."

"Stay here," I told Dean. Gritting my teeth, I took off.

"Liv, stop! You can't!" Dean yelled from behind me, but I moved out of his physical and blocking reach too fast. I placed my bet on the building being empty enough by now that I wouldn't get overwhelmed, hoping I could just reach Sway and Marigold in time.

As I hit the main hallway, I grabbed onto the doorframe, feeling that brick wall of emotions slam straight into me. I blinked several times and shook my head. I couldn't let it stop me. I blasted through flaming corridors, trying to use every bit of the fear rushing into my body, like if I could just spend the energy fast enough it wouldn't overwhelm me.

In the distance I could hear Dean yelling my name, and I had my own fear that he'd followed me in. But I kept going.

The stairwell was thick with smoke and smoldering piles of debris spotted the steps. I leaped over them, going so fast it was close to flight.

Bursting through the door to the second floor, I covered

my mouth with my sleeve. The smoke was so thick I could barely see. Flames rippled all over the ceiling.

I dashed down the corridor, dodging sparks and crumbled walls. I could barely see anything. Panic rose in me. *How am I going to find them?*

From behind me, I heard a bloodcurdling scream.

I skidded to a stop and backtracked to an intersecting hallway.

Silhouetted by the surrounding blaze I could see a person. I heard the voice of a man. He was holding a soft, round figure high above his head, a surge of rainbow energy vibrating around them, holographic against the flames.

The leech.

He had Marigold.

20

My heart whumped like it could burst from my chest.

On the ground was a much smaller figure—Sway, crawling toward me, screaming for help. "Monster! Devil!"

The man lowered Marigold down to where her feet barely touched the ground. Her head flopped limply. With a triumphant roar, he discarded her into the nearby flames.

My eyes went wide in terror. "NO!" I cried. It barely carried over the sound of the sprinklers, the alarms, the fire, and Sway screaming.

The silhouette grabbed Sway's ankle, pulling her back toward him. She slid along the floor, her fingernails clutching at the singed carpet.

The flames grew closer. They were immense, radiating so much heat it felt like my skin was melting. My senses swam, burning inside and out.

Sway flipped over onto her back and kicked at the leech, trying to scramble away. "Momma's not right. I'm not going to Hell! I won't!"

I could hear the strength in her kick as it collided with the man, but he didn't react at all. She was confused and untrained, didn't even know she had powers much less how to use them against the multi-powered leech.

I pulled my soaked cardigan off and dropped it to the ground. Mustering my speed, I barreled down the smoky corridor. I slammed my forearm across the man's throat, trying for a blow to his windpipe, trying to incapacitate him more in the already hard-to-breathe environment.

If nothing else, my appearance seemed to stun him. He dropped Sway and took a few steps back, all blurry, shadowy shapes in the smoke.

I looked down at her. "Get out of here!"

Her brow was furrowed and she looked at me with barely open eyes that streamed with tears.

I reached to help her to her feet, ready to carry her if I had to.

A hand grabbed the back of my neck. It slammed me down to the ground.

I landed hard beside Sway. I flipped, jumped to my feet, swung and missed.

The leech was fast. Too fast. Too strong. Something hard cracked against my shoulders and sparks flew all around. I smelt singed hair. I could barely see a thing. My eyes and throat stung with each wheezing breath.

I took another blow to the back and landed next to Sway again, who was mumbling prayers and crawling away. I tried to look but couldn't see where the leech was. The smoke was so thick now I doubted he could see where we were either.

I scooped Sway up into my arms and, using every last bit of speed I had, I dashed back the way I had come, careening into walls, rolling down stairs, and stumbling over ash-covered floors. Only sheer momentum kept us going.

We reached the ground floor, and I almost crumpled. Everything was too much. It was a struggle to put one foot in front of the other, but I kept going. *We have to get out.* I spotted a pale white square of light up ahead and hoped it was the exit. I hobbled blindly toward it and soon, the cooling effect of Dean's presence washed over me. I headed toward that feeling, and almost cried in relief as though he could heal every burn

I'd received.

I stumbled out the exit with Sway in my arms.

I wasn't sure where we were but there was fresh air, and I felt Dean beside me, taking Sway out of my arms. He wasn't a proesthian, but he was strong enough to carry her petite body.

My vision cleared slowly, but faster than a regular human's would have, I imagined. We were in a side strip between the main building and an outdoor covered area. Sway had wrapped both arms tight around Dean's neck, almost entirely supporting her own weight as she clung to him.

I drank deep gulps of air into my charred lungs, basked in a few seconds of relief, then turned back towards the building.

"What are you doing? The whole place is going to collapse on itself. You can't go back."

"Marigold is still in there. The leech got her. She's *in the fire*. I have to save her."

Dean grabbed my wrist. I could feel his blocking power kick in hard and my strength sapped away. He wasn't letting me go anywhere.

"If she's in the fire it's already too late." His voice was rough from the smoke. "Don't be the hero who dies."

I tried to pull away, but I couldn't gather the strength. Tears welled in my eyes and I dropped onto my knees.

He was right. But it *hurt*.

Behind me I heard a loud slam. A figure stumbled out of an entrance at the other corner of the building, a black mask covering his face and hair. As I spotted him, he spotted us. The leech. He stood in the rain of ash and stared at the three of us long and hard.

I stood, ready to fight.

"Olivia! Dean!" a woman yelled.

I spun around. It was the lead agent from the convention center. She had bright pink hair and a scar across her chin. Half a dozen plain-clothed agents from Limbus ran up behind her, identifiable only by the matching tracker bands they all wore.

"The leech," I yelled. "He's—"

I turned back to find the space he'd been standing empty. *Gone.*

The lead agent signaled with her hands and three of her team split off, flashing away with empath speed in search of the man.

"Are you hurt?" She checked me over, eyes lingering over my ash-grayed skin and red welts, then glanced over Dean, still cradling Sway.

"Is this one of them?" she asked.

"Yes. Sway," I gasped between coughs. "Marigold … he just

... he threw her in the flames."

The agent nodded slowly, and wrapped an arm carefully around me, leading me away from the devastation. She spoke to her team. "Let's get the kids safe."

Dean handed Sway over to one of the agents and they took us around to a van, which I got into gratefully. It felt like some of my burns were already healing, but I was wrecked.

Dean took a seat beside me and held my hand. "I was so worried I was going to lose you."

I leaned back against the headrest. "I'm sorry. I know that was a bit crazy, but I couldn't leave them in there."

"Don't apologize. You did you. You're a hero, through and through, Livvy. Ever since I first met you. Worrying I'll lose you comes naturally with that." Dean looked down at our joined hands. "But weirdly, I think it's helping me. Each time things get dangerous, but you come through okay, I build a bit more hope. But beyond that it reminds me how fragile life is, and that *I* have to come to terms with it. I can't control everything, or hide from everything, and blocking it all out means I just miss out on the good things too. Does that make sense?"

My tears flowed again, cleaning my eyes. "Yeah. A lot of sense. I get scared of losing you too. When Emma pulled that gun the other day ..." I gulped back a sob and rested my wet cheek on

Dean's shoulder. "Maybe I'm really not cut out for this."

Dean let go of my hand and wrapped both arms around me. There was a rigidness to his embrace that told me he still struggled between releasing his emotions and holding back, probably for my sake. I still snuggled into his awkward hug. "No. You saved Sway today. You identified her, you realized the threat, and you saved her life entirely. You're amazing."

I couldn't save Marigold though. The leech was one hundred percent monster, taking what he wanted then throwing away the rest. And the way he had looked at us …

He knew our faces now. It felt like only a matter of time before he was discarding our used-up shells like we were nothing.

21

We were rushed into Limbus and straight to medical. Limbus only had one ward area, so we ended up on beds at the end of the room where the drained were, sectioned off only by curtains.

Dr. Crossman, Felix and a group of nurses were there, ready for action. Sway and I were covered in ash and burns, but were already recovering well on our own, thanks to our proesthian-enhanced healing. The team still got us to change our ruined clothes. They cleaned us up, spread medicated gels over the raw patches of skin, and made us sit breathing pure oxygen from masks for a while. When they found out we'd had physical contact with the leech, they checked our hands and under our nails for signs of his DNA, and sent our clothes to Felix's lab for forensics.

Sway stayed quiet the whole time, listening to Mr. Crossman explain to her the gist of what was going on. About empaths, proesthians, leeches, emotions and powers, and soon her face clouded over. It wasn't the same enthusiastic reaction I'd had when I first found out about empaths. Of course, I hadn't been in the psych ward for years being told I was crazy beforehand.

Dean had minor burns on one hand from when he'd tried to open a hot door handle and, without proesthian healing powers to help his lungs, he was going to have to stay on oxygen a lot longer than we did.

Felix also took my phone from me, promising to use his genius powers to get it going again after its dousing, then returned soon with it sitting in a bowl of uncooked rice. He left, the rest of the medical staff not far behind him.

Dr. Crossman called my parents, had a quick chat to them, then handed her phone over to me. I pulled my oxygen mask to the side.

"Livvy, honey, I'm so glad you're okay. Terry called a while ago and told us the facility was on fire." Mom's voice was frantic. Dad spoke too. They must have been on speakerphone together. "We've been trying to call you ever since."

I glanced at my phone sitting in the bowl of rice on the bedside table, hoping it wouldn't have to be replaced again. "Yeah, the fire started just after our sessions finished. But we got out okay. A bit smoky and dirty, but we're all fine. Limbus just want to keep us here for observation a bit longer."

I heard a loud sniffle. "We're on our way, okay? We'll be there soon. We love you, Lollipop."

"Love you too, Mom and Dad."

"Tell Dean he's growing on us, too," Dad added.

I smiled. "Will do."

When I hung up and handed the phone back to Dr. Crossman, a movement caught my eye. From the doorway, Emma peeked in. She had a hand pressed onto her chest and a frown on her face. She caught me watching and her mouth opened a little then closed again. She frowned even deeper and disappeared.

Dr. Crossman took her phone and left too. Now they had more information on the leech, and he was growing so bold in his attacks. They were doing everything they could to find him.

I lay still for a while, breathing through the mask and doing every calming exercise I knew to release the tension from my body.

The ward was silent—almost too silent.

I rolled my shoulders and looked around the room. I could see Jake, Jamie, and Donny a few beds down. They lay on their backs, faces blank, hands resting by their sides. Mr. Kairu and the others I didn't know were also there.

Next to them was Holbrook, the man who had fallen into the coma before the fire started. Apparently, a nurse had gotten his bed down the emergency elevator before the sprinklers went off. The agents managed to do whatever they'd needed to take possession of someone who was a patient at a mental institute. I imagined the details were for them to know, and for me to act like I'd never heard.

In the bed to my right, Dean had dozed off. I envied him. There was no way I was getting some rest with these *bodies* all around us. I stared at the lines of his face for a while, but he remained so still it brought me no comfort. He lay face up, hands by his sides, just like the bodies. Fear clogged my throat.

I turned the other way. The bed to my left was empty, the sheets folded back where Sway had been. When had she left? I pushed myself up into a sitting position, looking for her. She couldn't have gone far; the staff would have never let her leave the premises.

Still, she'd gone *somewhere*. Unable to find rest either, probably. Every time I closed my eyes, I could see Marigold's body being flung into the fire. I hated it. I wanted the image out of my head.

I pulled back my covers and stepped down into a pair of slippers a nurse had given me along with the pale blue scrubs I wore, slightly too big for me and rolled at the waist.

Quietly, I moved to the doorway, wary about going too far from Dean. There was no sign of Sway out the main door; the hallway was empty. There was another door leading to a fire escape. She might have taken that. I stood on tiptoes to look out the small, high window in the ward. Below, I could see the stormwater drain that ran across the back of the Limbus property, and a tiny figure sitting on the edge of it.

I calculated the distance with my eyes. I should be okay that far from Dean. It was one floor down, but only a pathway width distance between the building and where Sway sat.

I pushed through the heavy fire door and tiptoed down the plain concrete stairs.

Sway turned to me when the external door closed with a thud. She sat on the weed-cracked concrete, her knees tucked up to her chest.

With my hands shoved into the shallow front pockets of my pants, I walked toward her with care. I didn't want to spook her. I had no idea where her head was at after everything.

As I sat down beside her, she gave a partial smile. "Can't rest either?" she asked.

"Nope."

She nodded, her eyes dark. "Monsters make it hard to sleep. I've met monsters before."

Down the slope of the wide drain channel, a small shadow moved. A rat, poking its head out of a grate. Sway leaned forward, pulling her legs down into a cross-legged position. She reached into the front of her scrub shirt and into her bra, pulled a cookie out, and tore off a crumbly piece. She threw it near the rat. The rat spooked at first, then eased toward the morsel, took it in its little claws, and ran back for cover.

"Tastes too salty smoky now," Sway said, breaking more pieces and throwing them down into the channel. "Sorry I got so clingy with your man."

"Oh, that's okay?" She caught me off guard. I hadn't thought twice about it at the time, having just escaped a catastrophic fire and death.

"His, *blocking*, is it? I just really needed it. I needed to feel *less* then, after feeling *everything*." Sway looked so small.

"I get it. And I really didn't think anything of it. Guess I'm not the jealous type." I also trusted Dean. A rush of warmth filled me. *I love him so much. I have to tell him.*

"You realize how good it is to know I'm not alone in feeling this way? That I'm not a nut nougat brain? At least, not completely." Sway tilted her head back, looking up at the dusk-tinted sky. "I used to take Marigold up onto the institute roof sometimes, just her and me. I liked being able to feel nothing but her golden light. And it was the only time I could get her to talk, when it felt like just me, her, and the sky. I don't know how she managed to stay so happy. I wish she could have known, too. That she wasn't crazy."

My eyes stung, too dry for more tears. I closed them and saw Marigold, the leech, the flames. "I'm sorry you lost your friend. I wish I could have saved her."

Sway swatted then scratched the side of her head. "There are worse ways to go. Mr. Crossman said that when this leech thing drained her, she fell into a coma. She wouldn't even have felt the fire."

I tried to see the comfort in that, but it was hard.

Sway tossed the last of the crumbs down into the drain then wiped her hands on her scrub-covered thighs. She looked back to the building, but didn't make any move to return to it. "Empaths, huh? All these slippery, shiny emotions … I never used to know what was really real before. Nobody else seemed to *feel* the way I did." She turned her hands over and smacked one palm to the other. "There were times when I thought my emotions would make me burst like popcorn. Or I would get so sad…" She trailed off for a moment and then picked up again. "So sad I felt like I could swallow the world with my grief."

I shivered, folding my arms tight around my chest. I knew that feeling. That was how I'd felt when I stole the life force from Jake and the others. Like I could have swallowed them whole.

Sway reached her hands up toward the evening star, the first pale sparkle in the still bright sunset. "When I was angry, I just knew if I reached up, I could tear down the sky."

She pulled her fists closed and down to her chest. "But then they would drug me up and I would relax. And all the rainbow light would just simmer out of my pores."

"I'm glad we were able to get you here safely. Now Limbus can help you, train you, teach you."

She let her hands fall into her lap and looked at me with a thin smile. "I wonder where my life would be if I'd known before now. If I could have done anything to control myself enough to stay on the sane side of the line. My own parents tucked me away so they wouldn't have to look at all my feelings every day."

I thought of my mom and dad, probably still on a train on their way to me. "My parents have been pretty cool with it.

I'm really lucky to have them, especially with the incredible stuff-ups and ridiculous danger I've been in. I'm surprised we all haven't short-circuited our emotional systems. I've been hot mess after hot mess even with a great support network. Being an empath can be a bit extreme. So yeah, welcome to the team?" I chuckled wryly.

Sway cracked a small smile. She rested one fist on her hip and put her other straight out in the air. "With our powers combined, we are the Emotional Wrecks!"

We both broke out into relieved, hysterical giggles. It felt good to let it all out, as though the laughter healed me as much as the tears I'd run dry.

Non-funny thoughts returned quickly though. Because I did have powers combined. Powers I needed to return. Although …

I gasped.

Sway jumped. "What is it?"

I put my hand out, touching her arm like she was a savior. "What you just said, about combining empath powers. You gave me an idea." Chewing my lip, I ran the thought over and over again in my head. It was definitely something. Something we could try. Something that might actually work. I kept my mouth closed, not wanting to jinx it.

I hopped to my feet and Sway looked up at me, confused.

"Good idea? Bad idea?"

I stared off down the length of the storm drain, spaced out, worried, and hopeful.

Sway stood up in front of me and tapped her finger to my forehead.

My eyes met hers, and a smile reappeared at the corners of my lips. "An idea of how to put the drained empaths back into their bodies again."

22

On our way back to the ward, Sway detoured and flagged down an agent to send for the Crossmans and Rayni.

When we reached the ward, Rayni was already there, sitting cross-legged on the end of her brother's mattress, talking to him softly.

Sway returned to her bed as though she'd never left.

I rushed over to Rayni, full of enthusiasm. When I got closer, I could see the blue aura surrounding her in the dim light, and even more clearly, the tears on her cheeks. I didn't want to get her hopes up too much in case this didn't work. I reined myself back in. Leaning my hip on the side of the bed,

I cautiously explained my plan. I had to get her to understand it because she was the key component. She and I had to work together to make it happen.

Her young round face watched me intently as I tried to explain the concept, still so new and nebulous, even in my own mind. I was worried she wouldn't get it at all, but a bright sparkle of comprehension flared in her eyes. When I finished, she looked up and away for a moment as though doing math in her head.

"Actually, it could work," she said, with a small, cautious smile. She reached down and squeezed her brother's foot through the blanket.

Dean had woken up while we'd talked. He took his oxygen mask off and came over beside us. He stood there with his arms crossed, his face straight, as always. He probably wasn't thrilled at the idea of waking up the guy who'd shot him. Neither was I, but that wasn't the point. If this could be done, there was a chance to save everyone. We just had to trust that Limbus could manage Jake, Jamie, and Donny appropriately once they were awake again.

The Crossmans arrived at the same time, and had brought Felix with them.

"No luck on a clean DNA sample yet," Dr. Crossman reported.

"Have you thought of some other detail about the leech that could help? Is that why you called us?"

I shook my head and pointed at the three boys. "I was talking to Sway, and she gave me an idea. An idea of how I could return their powers. I want to try it now."

Felix's face lit up with excitement, but Dr. Crossman was more hesitant. "Let's hear the idea first."

I walked to the foot of Jake's bed, not even wanting to look at him, but it was necessary. "We combine powers. I was watching Rayni the other day, and I could see how the emotions flowed from her and through other people when she pushed them out with her emogen abilities. I think those powers could help me push out all of this inside me."

Dean spoke softly. "Would you be able to do that without pushing out your own … self?"

"I think so. In the fire, I was able to channel and sort the emotions I was feeling into unique streams to find our way out. We know from the tests there are four distinct patterns in my head, and now I'm focusing on those, I can really feel them. I can feel who they are, their energy, which one is which."

Dr. Crossman's normally unflappable expression looked close to tears, but her voice remained steady. "And you want to try this now?"

I nodded, keeping my eyes from making contact with Dean's. "I want to be just me again, so things can be at least more normal in some ways. I do have one concern, though."

All eyes were on me, waiting. I puffed out a breath. "The leech was strong. So strong, and so fast. Sway, or probably any normal empath, couldn't stand a chance. Even as I am, all charged up, I could barely hold him off. I was only just fast enough to get away. I'm worried we need this"—I held my fists up in front of me—"this extra power I have, or we won't have any way to fight the leech."

Dr. Crossman shook her head adamantly. "Olivia, I admire your bravery but it's not your job to fight him. It never should have been. Leave it to the grown-ups and let yourself just be you."

Dean took my hand and I looked up into his face, still smudged with ash. His gray-eyed gaze was intense, making me shiver. "You're more than enough on your own. For anything."

I wanted to kiss him. But the kissing would have to wait.

And if this worked, that wait wouldn't be long.

"Okay. Okay, should we start?" I gestured to Rayni who came to stand behind me. "I've already talked it all over with Rayni."

"One more thing first," Mr. Crossman said. He took his wife's hand and they nodded to each other. "Assuming this works, Dean, we want you to block the three boys permanently as soon as they are awake."

My mouth popped open. I had hoped Limbus would do what was needed to deal with the three of them, but hadn't expected they would choose that path. Maybe it was easier for them to decide, since they were blocked themselves. After they were disowned by their own sons, maybe they thought there really was no hope for them.

"What about second chances?" I asked, unsure.

"We don't have the resources for second chances right now—not with having to focus everything on the leech." I could hear pain in Dr. Crossman's voice. "Jake and Jamie, with everything we've taught them? They could be a huge risk in so many ways. Even once blocked, we can't trust them not to continue pulling cons, or take revenge. We'll be sending them to regular authorities for their crimes as soon as it's safe to do so."

Mr. Crossman nodded. They'd clearly been over this together already and were firmly on the same page. "We'll help them how we can with legal aid and observation. If we feel there's a chance for them to turn their lives around with Limbus when the rest of the danger has settled, we can extract them from the legal system at that time."

Dean said, "Sounds like the best option to me." There was no emotion in his voice. I could only imagine everything running through his mind, given he was the major victim of one of the crimes the Crossman boys committed.

The Crossmans called a few agents up into the room just in case, and had me run over the finer details of my plan with Felix to see if it seemed sound. Felix smiled a wide, glittery smile, nodding along. He gave me a double thumbs up approval. "Oh boy, I can't wait to see this."

"Okay, Rayni. Showtime." I took position in front of the three beds the boys were lined up in.

Rayni came and stood beside me, her hands on either side of my back. "We'll do our best."

"Dean?" I found him with my eyes, standing to the side of the beds. "Can you drop your blocking on me? Completely? We need to let Rayni take control."

He frowned, then nodded. "You've got this."

A rush of nerves was the first thing I felt. Then a rush of emotions. The building was fairly empty and quiet, but even the controlled feelings of the Crossmans seemed extreme.

I gritted my teeth, then sensed Rayni's presence pushing through me. It cleared the emotions from me almost as fast as I could absorb them. My chest seemed to explode in a rainbow of colors.

I looked at the boys and closed my eyes, focusing on their

energies in my own body. Each energy was different. One, charming and gilded. Another, jittery and mischievous. The third, stoic and solid.

I moved my body into one of the meditation stances we'd been taught in training, and calmed my mind. I imagined each energy inside me as a stream, and then let them flow outwards with the current Rayni had created.

Sway gasped. *It's working. She can see it happening.*

I kept my eyes closed and focused.

I doubted anyone else could see the energy moving, but I could feel it escaping me. It was heavy, and the pressure on my chest grew. I spread my legs apart, stabilizing my body, and opened my eyes.

Tendrils of light flowed out of me toward the three I'd drained, and I could see the same vibration in the air I had seen around the leech and Marigold. My eyes watered and my lips peeled back as the pressure intensified, burning through me. I tried to hold my focus.

Jake began to stir. With a convulsion of my chest, the flow of light toward him ceased. He was back.

Dean was beside him instantly, shutting away his powers.

I couldn't slow the stream rushing through me. Jamie's light ended next. I grunted, releasing the last of Donny's energy, and the tendrils disappeared. But only *Sway* and I could see that.

Rayni kept pushing, and the flow through me cracked and fractured something inside. I came loose. I floated out of myself. I watched as Jamie and Donny's bodies twitched and woke. I watched as Dean shut them down.

I watched my body wobble and fall.

"Stop!" Dean yelled. He brought up his blocking ability and it flew over my body to Rayni's. I snapped back into my crumpling self.

Dean was there to catch me.

"Hey, hey, Liv? You okay?" He placed a hand on my cheek.

"Whoa." My head was swimming, something still loose, but everything felt like it was there. "Yeah, I'm here. All good. You don't have to block me so strong."

Dean furrowed his brow. "I'm not."

Looking back at Rayni, it was obvious from how she was plopped down on the floor, exhausted, that she wasn't using her powers on me either.

But I felt so … little.

I sat straight up, searching for signs of my powers.

There. I could sense the Crossmans' happiness and worry at the return of their sons. I could sense Rayni's relief and pride. I could sense Felix's joy and excitement. I could even sense a flutter of something warm coming from Dean.

I could no longer see emotions as colors. My powers were there, just smaller, back to what they once were. I had grown so used to the overwhelming excess, it took a while to remember what being *just me* felt like. "I may be totally less superhuman cool now, but it's so nice to just be me again."

Dean helped me to my feet; my legs were still shaky. He wrapped an arm around my waist for support. He smiled, one of those sparkling smiles I rarely saw from him. "You're still my superhero."

My cheeks grew hot, and I leaned into him, wrapping my arms around his waist too, feeling the warm flutter inside him growing.

"It really worked," Mr. Crossman sounded like he couldn't believe it. Dr. Crossman and Felix had both begun checking vitals on the three waking patients.

Rayni had taken a seat back on Ash's bed, watching him with a tired smile, and Sway watched from her own bed with her eyes and mouth wide open.

"What is going on? Where am I?" Jake's voice was harsh and croaky. His crusty eyes narrowed as he spotted Dean and me. "What did you do?"

I flinched and cuddled closer to Dean. How could I explain

everything I'd done? Everything that had happened and was happening?

Jake caught sight of his parents, and his pale skin flushed red. His eyes were wild with confusion as he took in the space, his brother, and Donny waking up beside him, and the other still unconscious patients.

Dr. Crossman started talking quietly to him, and Mr. Crossman beckoned Dean, Rayni, and I over. "Leave it to them now. You've done your part."

Rayni looked up at Mr. Crossman with wide, hopeful eyes.

He frowned back at her, gently. "You know we can't return your brother or the others until we get the leech in custody. This is a great reason to have hope though. We know now that it can be done. Thank you, Livvy."

"No problem." I shrugged, and yawned wide. It was still early evening, but I was exhausted.

Mr. Crossman's phone pinged and he checked the screen. "You parents have just arrived downstairs."

A wide grin split my face. I couldn't wait to see them. To go home.

My happiness was only tempered by knowing the leech was still out there. How did Limbus plan to catch the leech? And how could they make him do what I'd just done?

Although I wasn't as strong anymore, I felt proud of what I'd achieved, and somehow, that made me feel stronger. I was the heroine, walking into battle, ready to save the world. Somehow it felt like things were going to work out.

Beside me in the bowl of rice, my phone vibrated into life and dinged with missed calls and messages.

Felix barked a laugh. "Told you I was a genius!"

I smiled at my parents as I stepped out of the elevator and into reception.

Mom rushed toward me and grabbed me into her arms. She let out a cry of affection. "Oh, I was so worried. I can't believe there was a fire. Of all the things we have to worry about, some random fire happens." She brushed my still ashy hair from my face and kissed my forehead.

I realized Limbus hadn't said anything to them yet about the leech being there, and that maybe the fire wasn't so random after all. I would tell them later, after the other news. Maybe after a shower and some sleep.

Dad stepped forward. "Uh, Livvy? Where's Dean? Shouldn't he be closer to you than this?"

Mom let me go just to arm's length, looking around for Dean too. I grinned at them both. "I don't need him to be close by anymore. I worked out how to return the extra powers. I'm back to normal me."

Mom's mouth popped open and she hugged me again. "That's wonderful! I know it's been hard for you, managing that."

"What about the boys? Are they actually awake?" Dad had just an edge of worry coming from him.

"It's okay. Limbus is dealing with them. I don't know if we'll even ever see them again." I explained what had happened, how Rayni and I had worked together, and the plan for the boys. "Dean blocked them all permanently—well, at least maybe permanently."

"Where's Dean now?" Mom asked. I loved that she seemed concerned for him as well.

"Well, that's what I mean by *maybe* permanently. Mr. Crossman asked if Dean could stay and work with Rayni to see if Dean could unblock the Crossmans. Now we have new options with combining powers they thought it was worth a shot." I yawned again, my mouth stretching wide, then smiled sleepily at my parents. "They said they'd only try a few things, what with all the other drama, but thought it was worth attempting ASAP since it would be super helpful if they had their powers again. I was going to wait with Dean and call you up to us, but he reminded me I don't have to always be near him anymore. He could tell how tired I was and said I should go home with you."

My heart still felt fluttery at the possibilities for Dean and I in our relationship now. And from the kiss we'd shared when he walked me to the elevator. From the words we'd spoken to each other. I knew we could be apart from each other now but I wanted to be closer to him than ever before. Although I also really wanted a shower and my own clothes and my own bed in my own home.

I started shuffling to the exit where a driver waited to take us to the train station. Mom and Dad walked on either side of me, keeping my slow, sleepy pace. Dad patted me on the back. "This should be really good for both of you."

"Does it feel weird not having Dean here?" Mom asked.

I looked up, as though I could see through the floors of the Limbus building to Dean. "Yeah. I'm so used to having him near me all the time. But that couldn't have gone on forever."

My mother smirked. "I get the feeling he would have done it forever if he had to."

My heart fluttered faster, part love, part fear. "Still, I didn't want him to feel obligated or forced to be with me. He needs his freedom, his own time. I want our closeness to be his choice."

Mom put an arm around my shoulder as we walked. "Damn, we raised you good."

I stuck my tongue out at her.

"What do you think he'll do now?" Dad asked. "You know, with all that free time."

"Take up knitting?" I shrugged. "I don't know. He said he'll come back home tonight, when they are done here. But long-term …"

A sharp sliver of doubt stuck like a splinter into my happiness. *What will Dean choose to do now?* I didn't want to doubt our relationship, but just moments after we were able to be apart, he'd sent me away. I shook the feeling off. I was just overwhelmed. I couldn't doubt him after what we'd just shared.

"He might want to go home," Mom said gently. "Regardless of his father's failings as a parent, family is family. Or maybe Limbus has room for him, like the other kids who board here. But if Dean wants to—and I don't know how your father feels about it, but as far as I'm concerned—he's more than welcome to stay with us as long as he wants."

"He's a good kid," Dad said in agreement.

I blinked tears from my weary eyes. "Yeah, he is."

We stepped out of the main doors. I stared down at the slippers on my feet, not even caring I'd be riding the train looking like this. The driver was Mr. Graybiel again, and he gave me a less nervous, warmer smile when he dropped us off at the train station.

I dozed on and off along the way home, leaning my head on Dad's shoulder, my mom's arm still supporting me.

I felt the separation from Dean like I'd been cleaved in two, and insecurity continued to build the longer we were apart. I was afraid that he wouldn't want to come back to our house. Maybe living at Limbus was the best choice; it would probably be really good for him. It would be selfish of me to not let him make that choice.

But I wanted to be selfish. I wanted to be the teenage girl all over her teenage boyfriend, and for the first time, I finally could be. I didn't want to be apart from him at all.

But being a teenage girl and having normal teenage worries seemed distant to me now. I wasn't the same Livvy I was when I'd been handing out blankets at the shelter. I wasn't even the same Livvy who was in the park that night with Jake's gang, fighting for my life and Dean's. And I couldn't expect Dean to be the same either. I just hoped that our new, different selves worked as well together as our old selves did.

When we got off the train, we got a taxi from the station back home, and I went straight into the shower to wash away the smoke and ash from my hair and skin.

I wobbled into some soft, clean pajama pants and a T-shirt. When I crawled into bed, I pulled my knees to my chest and wrapped my shirt over them down to my ankles, cocooning myself.

Mom knocked on the door and came in, pulling the blankets up and tucking me in. She smiled a warm, motherly smile. "You've been through quite a bit, *again*. Get some sleep."

My eyes flashed to hers and I sucked in my lips.

She smirked. "When Dean gets back, I'll poke my head in and let you know."

She could read me perfectly. "Thanks, Mom."

It was only just past nine, and I tried to wait up for Dean anyway. Yawning, I closed my eyes and remembered the moment we'd shared saying goodbye at Limbus, feeling every tingling touch, reliving every joy-soaked word …

Dean held my hand and walked me from the ward to the elevator. My whole being felt light, wobbly, joyous at just being *me* again. At finally ridding myself of the powers I'd stolen. I

221

grinned from ear to ear.

A smile spread slowly on Dean's lips as well, which made me even giddier. I kept throwing glances at those smiling lips of Dean's and warmth grew and grew inside me, and I could sense it from him too, being set free.

I pressed the elevator button, and turned to stand face-to-face with Dean. He took my other hand as well, holding both between us.

"Livvy. Everything … can be different now," he said softly, looking down at our hands.

I only had eyes for his lips.

He continued, "I'm going to make an effort not to push down my emotions anymore. It's going to be hard, but I'm ready. I'm ready to feel again. Feel everything. I think I have been for a while, but I've had to be careful."

For me. He has had to keep blocking everything away so he could keep me stable. I frowned, but he kept talking.

"But now, I want to allow myself to feel, to want, to fear. To *love.*"

I looked up into his gray eyes as a single tear rolled out of one, making me gasp. Never, *never*, not in all the tragedy or danger we'd been through, had Dean ever cried. Ever.

"Sorry," he said, almost automatically, shame in his eyes.

He reached a hand to wipe it away. I grabbed his wrist and stopped him.

"No. Never apologize for feeling. You can cry or laugh or do anything you need to do." I put my palm onto his cheek, holding the tear between us. "It's beautiful. *You're* beautiful."

Suddenly I was flooded with warmth and love. Streams of kind-heartedness, pride, and excitement flew through me, filling me to the brim. I could feel everything he had been blocking from himself for so long. I could feel how he still grieved for his mother, how he was saddened by but still loved his father, and lastly, his contentment at being close to me, his fear for my safety, and his overwhelming desire to be with me, in every possible way.

I stood up on my tiptoes and placed three quick, feather-soft kisses onto Dean's lips. I felt the smile on them grow, and then Dean grabbed me around the waist, pulling me into him and our kiss grew deep and strong. Every danger we'd shared, every loss and every fear, was washed away in a tidal-wave of *love* swirling around us.

The elevator dinged beside us. Doors opened and closed again. Dean lifted me from my feet and we spun in slow circles, our lips pressed hotly together.

Down the hall, Felix yelled at us to get a room.

Everything felt golden and sundrenched and like I could kiss Dean forever.

I slipped away from the memory and into sleep, swimming through the waves of visions I had seen over the last few weeks. Coming back to school and to Nati. Rayni's pale rainbow hair. Sway sharing a cookie with a rat. Ash's face fluttered by, smiling big at the bus stop. Dean hooked his fingers into mine.

But then things started to get dark.

I stood in the center of a pitch-black space. Red light grew as flames flickered all over walls on every side, boxing me in. Smoke rolled over my bare feet. I heard a striking laughter that made me sick to my stomach. Then, as if someone had stabbed me through the back and into my heart, a piercing pain took over me. My mouth fell open and I wheezed, only small moans escaping. The leech stood on all sides of me. So many of him. Moving so fast, surrounding me. He was everywhere and everything all at once and he was stealing my soul.

I struggled and fell backward onto the ground, tried to swim away through the smoke and darkness, but the leech was too fast. He grabbed me by my heart and lifted me high above his head. I looked down into his face and he seemed ... *familiar.*

I gasped awake, slippery with sweat. My eyes shot wide open and I sat straight up in the bed, grabbing at my chest. Looking around my room, I blinked in relief. It was a nightmare. Just a nightmare.

The clock on my phone's lock screen told me it was one in the morning. No other notifications were on the screen.

I frowned. Had I slept through Mom telling me Dean was back? He had to be here by now.

I picked up my phone, making sure there weren't any missed messages. I climbed out of bed and when I stepped out of my room, I noticed the light was still on in the kitchen. I squinted as I walked downstairs and into the light, seeing my parents still sitting at the kitchen table. Each with a coffee mug in one hand and a phone in the other.

"Why are you both still up?" I mumbled groggily. "Why didn't you wake me when Dean got back?"

Mom and Dad frowned, looking at each other, then back to me. "Lollipop, honey—"

Acid sickness rose in my throat. "He did get back, right? Where's Dean? Is he here? What's going on?"

A rush of sad worry spread from my mom to me. "Dean's missing."

<h1 style="text-align:center">24</h1>

"**M**issing?" I swallowed bile, unable to accept the concept. "He could still be at Limbus. Maybe they're just still trying things. Maybe they went later than they'd thought they would."

Even as I said it, I knew it couldn't be true. Rayni was already tired, so she couldn't have lasted this long.

"We called Limbus twenty minutes ago when we started getting worried. Dean left there at ten thirty."

"Then he should be back by now." I stepped left, then right, panic driving my actions, but I didn't know where to turn. I glanced again at the phone in my hand—no messages from Dean.

"Stay calm. Dean has his tracker. If something was wrong, he would have pressed the panic button. The trains might have just been held up. Limbus are checking."

My voice was louder than it needed to be. "Have you tried calling Dean?"

Mom bit her lip. "He's not answering."

"Lollipop ..." Dad put out a reassuring hand, but I was already moving.

Maybe it was nothing. Maybe he was just enjoying being free from me, on his own. Maybe his phone was flat. Maybe he was enjoying some complete solitude for a change. Maybe he'd fallen asleep on the train and missed his stop. Maybe, maybe, maybe swirled in my head but gave me no hope. I had to find him.

I ran for the front door, grabbing my red trench coat and throwing it on over my pajamas. I didn't take time for shoes. I dashed out onto the street, barefoot, while my parents yelled after me.

I built momentum, my feet slapping the tarmac on the empty roads. I sought and absorbed fear from every source I could to go faster. I drew in the fears from children's bedrooms where they had nightmares about monsters. I went faster, and faster, because I knew monsters were real. I prayed the monster hadn't gotten Dean.

The threat of the leech created an all-consuming fear within me. It was unlikely the leech would strike again so soon. It was unlikely the leech would know where Dean was. That was why Limbus had been fine with us taking trains home.

But the leech had seen our faces.

At the speed I was going, I would reach the train station in five minutes. I caught glimpses of myself in the shopfront windows as I passed, just a red streak flashing by. It didn't feel fast enough, and I wished I still had the three boys' powers as well.

My phone buzzed in the palm of my hand and I checked it quickly as I dashed down a side alley. It was Limbus.

I answered. "Do you know where he is?"

"Olivia." Dr. Crossman's voice was concerned. "Your parents told us you ran out to find Dean. We really need you to go back home where you'll be safe. We're activating your tracker until you get back."

"WHERE'S DEAN?" I yelled.

There was a shuffle and some mumbled voices. "We've activated tracking for him already, and I'm looking at Dean's location now. He's at the Bellscroft station—has been since we got your parents' call. We already have agents on the way to check, but he hasn't pressed his beacon or panic button. You really should go home."

I wasn't going home. I didn't hang up, but took the phone away from my ear, shoving it into my coat pocket.

I'm going to find Dean, sitting there just fine. He'll have fallen asleep waiting for a taxi at the station. He's just enjoying a moment alone. This is fine.

I ran faster.

The night air was icy and my breath burned cold through my chest and throat, but I didn't slow down. Greater than any fear I absorbed from my surroundings was my own terror, white-hot in my veins, pumping through me, pushing me even harder.

I rounded the corner to the train station.

The main entrance through the ticket turnstiles was all the way around the other side. A couple of drunks were arguing down the road. No one else seemed to be around as I looked through the chain-link fence at the platforms.

I clung to the fence with clawed fingers and leaned my head against the wire, staring through it for any sign of Dean.

Breath caught in my throat. Something flashed down in the gap on one of the tracks. The same way my tracker flashed now it had been activated.

I could hear a train in the distance.

Tightening my clawed grip on the chain-link fence, I tore it apart. I took off across the empty train station, leaping from platform to platform toward that flashing beacon.

The train was in sight now, heading for the track the flash had come from. I reached the platform and jumped down onto the tracks. I almost froze entirely when I saw … but I had no time to freeze.

My heart raced as I raced headfirst toward the train, toward the body between me and it.

The train's horn blared. It zipped past, clipping my elbow as it went by.

I stood on the platform again, shaking all over. Dean was lifeless in my arms.

I cried out as I slumped to my knees. *This can't be happening. Not now. It can't.*

I held my ear to Dean's chest, listening for his heartbeat. It was there, but slow, weak. Tears choked me as I stared at his pale and purple features.

"Dean? Dean, please wake up," I begged, but I knew there'd be no reply.

I pulled the phone from my pocket. All strength had left

me. I was numb, shivering, could barely breathe.

"Olivia? Olivia, are you there?" Dr. Crossman's voice was frantic.

I managed to get just one more sentence out before dropping the phone. "Dean's been drained."

CONTINUE READING LIVVY'S STORY IN EMOTIONALLY POWERFUL

A PERSONAL THANK YOU FROM SELINA

Thank you for reading my story, it means a lot to me to be sharing my magical worlds with you. As an indie author, receiving reviews and seeing people talk about my books are like receiving a big warm hug from my readers! Honest reviews help me improve as an author, and help bring my book to the attention of other readers. If you're enjoyed this book, please consider taking two minutes to leave a review at the online store you purchased this book. It really does mean the world to indie authors such as myself.

If you want to discuss the story or make sure I see your comments, just drop me an email at selina@selinafenech.com. I love to hear from readers, and reply to all personal emails!

SELINA A FENECH
BESHADOWED
DARKNESS UNKNOWN

SELINA A FENECH
BESHADOWED
BLOOD BOUND

SELINA A FENECH
BESHADOWED
SHADOWS AWOKEN

SELINA A FENECH
BESHADOWED
EVERDARK CURSED

MEMORY'S WAKE
SELINA A FENECH

HOPE'S REIGN
SELINA A FENECH

PROVIDENCE UNVEILED
SELINA A FENECH

EMOTIONALLY CHARGED
1
SELINA A FENECH

EMOTIONALLY UNSTABLE
2
SELINA A FENECH

EMOTIONALLY POWERFUL
3
SELINA A FENECH

ABOUT THE AUTHOR

Whether it's painting artworks or writing novels, creating fantasy works is Selina's biggest passion. She lives in Australia with her husband and daughter and loves food, gardening, geekery, and all things fantasy.

Find out more about Selina

Official website www.selinafenech.com

Facebook www.facebook.com/selinafenechart